GILL STEWART

Gemma's not sure

Sweet Cherry

Published by Sweet Cherry Publishing Limited
Unit 36, Vulcan House,
Vulcan Road,
Leicester, LE5 3EF
United Kingdom

First published in the UK in 2020
2020 edition

2 4 6 8 10 9 7 5 3 1

ISBN: 978-1-78226-481-1

Cover design by Rhiannon Izard

www.sweetcherrypublishing.com

Printed and bound in India
I.TP002

To Pia Fenton (aka Christina Courtenay),
great writer and fantastic friend.

Gemma

'I'm not sure I can do this.' I mean to say it inside my head.

'Of course you can!' Lily turns her gaze from my computer screen. 'You're the best singer in the school, and you're amazing at piano. You're bound to get–'

I wave my hand to shut her up, which works, surprisingly. Maybe she's noticed I'm on the verge of tears.

I mean, everyone seems to think I *should* do this. Go to uni, study Music, make a career out of it … They'd said it couldn't hurt to apply, could it? As it happens, yes, actually. Because now the Conservatoire has sent me details of the audition and just reading them makes me feel so sick I think I might need to run to the toilets. (This is saying something given the state of the ones at Galloway Academy.)

I take a deep breath and close the window.

'No need to think about it now,' I say, as brightly as I can.

'Of course not. Take your time. Although, the audition is in November, so you do need to decide fairly soon ...'

I pretend to rummage in my bag. Lily accepted her audition to study Drama straight away. No nerves at all. Me, I love singing at home, or in a choir – but on my own in public? My stomach lurches. And why did I even choose voice as a secondary instrument when I could have done just piano? Although, I'm not comfortable playing that in public, either.

Basically I'm pathetic.

Lily is being very patient, for her. She doesn't mention the audition again for at least two hours. Then, as we walk back to her house after school, she says, 'You know, they do a music-teaching course at the Conservatoire. Maybe you could consider that? It isn't so much about performing in front of people.'

'No, it's about performing in front of a class of kids every day of the year.'

'Only in term time.'

'Lily, I'm never going to be a teacher.'

She doesn't give up. 'You were really good when you led the choir in the pantomime last year. That was basically teaching. And you're a prefect. That shows you know how to use your authority.'

Lily's all about those 'transferable skills'. But, again, 'No, it shows I organise the prefect rota so I'm always on with you, and you can be the one to "use your authority".'

'Oh.' She looks surprised. Then she frowns. 'I thought it was because you enjoyed my company.'

'And that,' I add, in the unlikely event that I've hurt her feelings.

And I do enjoy Lily's company. She's been my friend for forever. And I'm usually good at tuning out her overenthusiasm.

As we turn to go up the steps to her front door I say, 'Anyway, why isn't Tom with us?'

'Tom and I don't spend our lives in each other's pockets, you know. We're both independent human beings.'

'But where is he?'

'Taking Sarah to her hospital appointment.'

'Ah.' That should put my worries about the Conservatoire into perspective. Tom's younger sister doesn't even get to go to school, so who knows if she'll ever be well enough for university? And yet …

What am I going to do about the audition?

Mrs Guthrie, my singing teacher, and Mrs Marshall, my piano teacher, will probably have something to say about it. I know Mum and Dad will just tell me to do what makes me happy, but that's the problem: I'm not sure what that is.

Jamie

Uni life is amazing! Freedom. No one looking over my shoulder all the time. No one planning what I should do every second. This is what I've been waiting for!

I'm not exactly smashing the academic side of things, but we're only a few weeks in. The social side will probably calm down soon – not that I want it to.

Innis, one of the guys in my flat, is on the same course as me and just as keen on making the most of student life.

'You coming over to the Union?' he says, as I drop my gym bag and reach for some juice from the fridge.

'Aye, why not?' I was going to look at my Accounting notes, but I've just put in a good training session. I deserve a break. 'Give me ten minutes for a shower.'

My phone rings as I head into my room. Mum, of course. I could just ignore it, but then she'll try again and again until she gets through.

'I'm in a bit of a hurry,' I answer.

'I won't keep you,' she lies cheerily. 'Just a couple of things. Your dad is in Glasgow tomorrow so he can take you out for dinner. That'd be nice, wouldn't it? And I wondered if you've got your marks back yet from your latest assignment? Are you refereeing this weekend? It'd be lovely if you could come home sometime soon but I know how busy you are–'

'Mum, that's already more than two things.'

'–and what I'm really phoning about is that Mrs Marshall has said she'll fit you in a for a long piano lesson before you take your exam. That's good of her, isn't it? If you let me know when you're coming home, I'll arrange it with her. Then we can discuss whether you want to go on and do the diploma.'

Shit. I'd forgotten I let Mum enter me for the Grade Eight piano exam. Grade Eight! Why she even thinks it's a good idea I have no clue. I've told her I have absolutely no desire to take my music further.

'Actually, Mum, I haven't been practising much – lack of access to a piano, you know – so maybe we should delay–'

'You can't do that! I've paid the entrance fee. Anyway, you need to pass this to count towards your Gold Duke of Edinburgh.'

Ah yes, that's why I'm still learning piano.

'I've got a lot on just now ...'

'I know you have, darling. So I won't keep you. Just message me a couple of dates and I'll arrange it all for you. Love you. Bye.'

That's another thing Mum's good at: ending conversations just when I'm about to get a word in.

Oh well. No point worrying about that now. I've got an evening's drinking to look forward to. Tomorrow is another day and all that.

The Finance lecture first thing the next morning turns out to be a group presentation. Which I knew about. Probably. At least before the evening in the Student Union, which turned out to be pretty good. Cheap beer, lots of laughs – what's not to like?

Aside from the headache as we saunter into the lecture room.

This guy Kris says, 'You okay to do the speaking, Jamie? You said you would if we put the slides together.'

'Yeah, fine.' I might have agreed to that. I'm too hungover to remember.

'You have looked over them, haven't you?'

'Of course.' I flash my most confident grin. 'Just having a final look now.'

I flick my laptop open and pull up the slides. I see someone was working on them at midnight last night, so I'm not sure when I was supposed to have had a chance to go over them. I was way too drunk by then anyway.

When it's our turn I straighten my shirt, check my reflection in a side window, and head to the front of the room. I've got this. If there's one thing I'm good at, it's standing in front of an audience and acting like

I know what I'm talking about. Dad says I get it from him. Lily, my ex, said it was an unfair advantage.

Whatever. We smash it. Looking confident really is half the battle. The lecturer nods throughout, and preens when I use some of his own phrases back at him. We even get a smattering of applause from the rest of the class, who pretty much slept through the other presentations.

Sometimes I have my doubts about this course. I mean, who actually enjoys Accounting and Business Studies? But right now, I'm on a high. The guys slap me on the back as we sit down.

I repeat: life is good.

Gemma

Ten days after I got the offer of an audition, I open the web pages of all the university courses I've applied to. I'm hoping that if I consider them quietly, in turn, I'll be able to decide which ones I really *want* to do. And I'm not going to base my decisions on which ones require an audition. Nope. Definitely not.

It is literally life-changing, deciding-the-course-of-my-future stuff, but half an hour in I am no further forward. In fact, I've migrated to social media, which *could* count as research since Jamie Abernethy is actually at university. And 'research' sounds so much better than 'stalking'.

It's a positive case study. Jamie's doing really well. Of course. Socialising like mad. Refereeing. People tag him in pictures all the time, in nightclubs or on football pitches. He's let his hair grow a bit and it suits him.

If I could be like anyone, I think I'd want to be like Jamie. He wouldn't be panicking about auditions. He doesn't stress about disappointing people – not that he ever could. He makes everything seem effortless. It must be nice to be like that.

As I scroll through, I just happen to notice that he's coming back to Newton St Cuthbert this weekend. That makes me sit up. Not that it's anything to do with me. It's just that Mrs Marshall has asked me to go in for an extra lesson too – "summoned" is the word Jamie uses.

Maybe I should take up that Saturday slot she's been going on about. Mrs Marshall says it'll be good preparation for the Conservatoire audition. I still haven't told her that I probably won't be going to it. I haven't told anyone.

On Saturday morning it starts snowing. In the first week of November!

I hate snow. It's cold and wet and inconvenient and – okay it's quite pretty, but otherwise I hate it. It's dangerous. There'll be cars sliding off the road and old people falling and breaking their hips. People should just stay indoors on days like this. Instead, I'm heading to Mrs Marshall's.

We could have cancelled. I'm sure someone sensible like Jamie will have cancelled. But Mum said we couldn't because it would be rude and the weather's not *that* bad. I insist we leave early, so at least we have plenty of time for me to drive very veeeery slowly out of town, towards the village where Mrs Marshall lives. And yes, I am driving. Mum thinks it'll be good practice for me.

There are a surprising number of tracks on the road. I wonder if those other drivers also had appointments to keep, or if they were just going shopping or something. People can be so reckless.

Then I see a car at a crooked standstill ahead of us.

'Brake gently!' shouts Mum, when I brake so hard we start to skid.

I ease off and we come to a gradual halt on the road, and not in the deeper snow at the side, which is where the car in front of us has ended up.

'That's Jamie's car,' I say, and a wave of horror washes over me. Technically it's Jamie's parents' car, but– 'What's happened? Is he hurt?'

I jump out. At that moment the door of the car in front opens and a familiar figure climbs slowly out. Thank goodness.

'Jamie! Are you okay?'

Jamie leans against the open door. He doesn't look at me. 'Shit. That gave me a fright.'

'Are you okay?' I say again.

'Not if Dad sees what I've done.'

'Can I help?' I say, with no idea how I could actually help.

I manage to reach him without slipping over, but Mum comes up behind me and hasn't allowed a safe stopping distance. She careens into my back. 'Watch out!'

I grab hold of Jamie to keep myself upright, then blush furiously and let go. 'Sorry, sorry.'

'I don't suppose you've got a shovel?' says Jamie. He doesn't seem to notice that I was briefly pressed against him, but my heart has kicked up a notch. 'If we can clear a bit of snow, I should be able to get some traction.'

'Maybe,' I say doubtfully. There's an awful lot of snow on the road, and one of his front wheels is in the ditch.

'We don't have a shovel,' says Mum.

I wish someone else were here. Say Lily, or Donny – or better still, Donny's older brother Karl. He's a traince mechanic. He'd probably have a tow rope. But there's just us, which Jamie seems to realise now as he looks at me and Mum properly.

'Sorry, did I say hello? Hi Gemma, Mrs Anderson.'

'Hi,' I say. Mum nods.

Jamie says, 'If we push from the front we might get it back on the road.'

The snow is falling lightly now but the stuff on the road is compacted and slippy. I'm not sure this is a great idea, but what do I know?

'Are you all right?' Mum asks.

'I think so.' Jamie shakes his head so that the resting snowflakes scatter. 'Yeah, I'm fine. It's the car I'm worried about.' He looks between us: two complete lightweights. 'It might be better if I push. Will one of you get in and steer?'

Mum nudges me. 'You're the lightest. You'd better get in, and I'll help Jack push.'

"Jack" and I exchange a look. I don't want to be at the steering wheel, and Jamie doesn't want to be at the front of the car next to my impractical mother. She might be curvier and therefore heavier than me, but she's wearing heels – which were a bad idea even before this happened. I, meanwhile, am dressed sensibly in jeans and flats.

'I'll push,' I say.

It takes us about a hundred attempts, not helped by me apologising every time my hand touches Jamie's over the bonnet. Finally, we get the car back on the road. Mum jumps out and rushes round to look, as if she can diagnose any problems.

'Let's move before the snow gets heavy again,' says Jamie. 'Go slowly and don't brake suddenly. That's what made me go off the road in the first place. I was trying to avoid something that ran out. A cat, maybe.'

I love that he was worried about a cat, and now about us. I haven't time to savour it now, but I store it up for later.

'I'm heading to Mrs Marshall's,' says Jamie. 'What about you?'

'We're heading there too,' says Mum. 'What a coincidence.'

Jamie

What the hell? Why did Gemma Anderson and her mum have to be driving along this particular road at that particular time? I was an idiot to brake like that. Be nice if there'd been no one around to witness the result. Although, I suppose I did need help getting out of the ditch.

At least the car doesn't seem to be damaged. I might not even need to tell Dad what happened.

I lead the way to the village where Mrs Marshall lives, driving ultra-carefully. I'm late for my lesson, but Gemma is way too early for hers. It's typical of her, though. I remember her being a worrier. She'd probably rather be twenty minutes early than five minutes late.

When we arrive her mum says, 'We could do a bit more driving practice, while we wait until your friend has finished.'

Gemma shakes her head firmly. 'No way. I'm not

driving any further in this weather. If even Jamie can skid off it's way too dangerous.'

It's nice of her to make out like I'm a good driver, but she must have realised I took that corner too quickly, cat or no cat.

Mrs Marshall puts an end to the discussion by ushering the Andersons into the sitting room and leading me to the music room at the back of the house. They're still too close for my liking. I really haven't practised lately. I make tons of mistakes, and I'm sure Gemma and her mum can hear every single one.

Mrs Marshall shudders as I struggle through the Shostakovich. 'I know this is a challenging piece,' she snaps, 'but it's not beyond your capabilities. Let's go over it again.'

I nod and do what she says, agreeable and pleasant. Inside I'm pissed off that I'm here, making a complete fool of myself.

Eventually I finish and make a quick escape. I tell Mum that the lesson was good but that I definitely need to practise more. Then I shut myself in our dining room with the piano for a couple of hours. My playing is half-hearted at best. I'm more than ready to be distracted by news that some guys from my year at school are also home for the weekend. We arrange to meet up. It'll be good to find out how they're doing at uni, although I might keep quiet about the fact that I've failed my first two assignments. I haven't told Mum and Dad yet either. I don't want them (her) freaking out.

Gemma

I'm standing in the foyer of the poshest hotel I've ever been in, wondering why I let Lily drag me here. Sarah is looking a bit overawed too. Lily is beaming.

'Sometimes my dad actually does something useful! Family membership of a spa, with vouchers for guests – I can live with that.'

'I didn't even know this hotel existed,' says Sarah, gazing around at oak panelling set off by massive tropical flower displays and very fancy wallpaper.

Lily waves her hands as though she created the whole thing. 'It's been here forever, but they did a big revamp last year and added on the spa and leisure centre. Come on, we go this way.'

She leads us through double doors and we move from old-fashioned opulence to clean modern lines made from metal and glass. It smells of money and I don't belong. Plus I can see a *massive* swimming pool through the wall of glass.

'I'm not sure about this.' Lily promised I wouldn't have to swim, but I don't know if I can trust her. She has that slightly manic look in her eyes like when she has a *plan*.

'It's going to be brilliant. Just the place to be on a freezing November Sunday. Let's get changed and then I'll show you around.' She flashes her membership card at the girl at the desk, who looks more like a model than a receptionist, and scoops up three beautifully rolled fluffy towels. This is nothing like the local Newton St Cuthbert pool.

Lily pushes open the door to the changing room. 'Come on. There's a sauna and a steam room and a hot tub and all sorts.'

'Lead the way,' says Sarah, grinning. I'm pleased that she's pleased.

I take out my costume, which I haven't worn in years. It's a basic navy blue one-piece and it's going to look completely out of place here. Part of me is hoping it won't fit, but it does. Apparently I'm just as skinny and almost as flat-chested as I was when I was twelve. Lucky me.

'I'm not swimming,' I repeat to Lily, hiding myself in the wonderfully soft towel.

'Not if you don't want to.'

'I don't want to.' Sometimes it's best to handle Lily by avoiding the discussion, but today I need to meet her head on.

'That's fine, that's fine. Come on, let's shower first.

They have all sorts of buttons you can press: tropical rain and scented air and I don't know what.'

As we follow Lily, Sarah says quietly, 'You okay?'

I must look really worried if she's asking that. I should be the one concerned about her. This is a big excursion by her standards.

I nod and put on my best smile.

The thing Lily doesn't understand is that I'm not *nervous* of water; I'm completely and absolutely petrified of it. I know it's silly. I can swim (a length of the tiny Newton St Cuthbert pool). I know as long as I'm not out of my depth, I can put my feet down and I'll be fine. There's no current here to drag me away. No soft sand to suck me down. But still …

We try the steam room, and the sauna – although only briefly in case the heat is too much for Sarah. We rest for a bit and Lily insists Sarah drinks some water, then I let them persuade me into the hot tub. It makes me feel sick, the swirling, and not being able to see the bottom. But there's a ledge to sit on and I can hold on to the rail. The water is almost hot so it's more like a big bath tub than a pool. I close my eyes to see if it's better when I can't see the frothing water. It isn't.

'You two should go and swim,' I say, hoping I don't sound as breathless as I feel. 'I can lie on one of those recliners and watch you.'

'Soon,' says Lily dreamily, letting her legs float up in front of her. 'Isn't this bliss?'

'I love it,' agrees Sarah. She's not even holding on to the side. She rolls over onto her front and then onto her back again. I know it's not deep but she could have gone under. She really could.

My heart is pounding as I hold very firmly on to the metal rail and feel for the steps with my feet. I'm okay. I can just climb out, nice and slow and calm.

'Don't go yet,' says Lily, sitting forwards and sending a wave of water towards me. I grab at the rail with my other hand.

I'm on the top step when three middle-aged women come across so I have to move to let them in. I don't need to answer Lily. The hot tub is a bit crowded now. Lily pulls a face at Sarah and they both follow me out.

I wrap myself in my lovely towel and lie down. Lily and Sarah start splashing around in the pool. Lily's a strong swimmer but she's not doing any lengths with Sarah around.

I'm alone and almost dry, but I don't feel comfortable here. I don't like the echoey noises, the constant sound of water. But I'm okay. I've come here and I've been in the hot tub, and soon, hopefully, we can go home.

After a while, Lily comes and sits sideways on the neighbouring lounger. I know it's her even though I keep my eyes closed. I've been expecting it.

'Don't you think it would be good to *try* a bit of swimming?' she says.

I can't suppress a shudder. 'No.'

'I think maybe you need to challenge yourself, you know? If you got used to the water, then this fear wouldn't have such an impact on your life.'

'It doesn't have an impact on my life. I don't go swimming. Simple.'

'Gem, you don't even paddle when we're at the beach. It's holding you back.'

I open my eyes so I can glare at her. 'I can't think of a single thing I want to do with my life that involves water or swimming. It is not holding me back.'

'But it would be so good for you to face your fear ...'

It might be good for someone like Lily to face their fears (if she has any). It'd take me forever to get through all mine.

'Didn't you say they do good milkshakes in the restaurant here? I think I might get dressed and go try one.'

I stand abruptly. The recliner doesn't even wobble. Everything in this place is perfect.

'Gem–'

'I'll see you when you're finished. No hurry.'

I don't run across the tiled floor, because then I might slip, but I walk as fast as I can. Once I've pushed open the door to the ladies' changing room, and let it fall shut behind me, I feel like I can breathe properly for the first time today.

I've been dreading this visit. If it were just me and Lily I would have backed out, or not even said yes to begin with. But Sarah was so excited and it's not like she gets to do much. I'd told myself that if I just didn't go in the swimming pool it would be fine. And it was, I guess. I mean, I didn't *drown*.

I sigh over my strawberry milkshake, and think some more about going for the Conservatoire audition. At least it wouldn't involve getting wet. With that in mind, it might just be doable. *Maybe*.

Possibly.

Jamie

I head back to Glasgow early on Sunday afternoon. It's a relief to get away from Mum. She's annoying enough on the phone, but when you're in the same house as her she's a complete nightmare.

I say I need to get back because I've got a football match to ref, which is true – it's just not until eight this evening.

When I reach halls there's no one around. I'd been hoping to waste a bit of time chatting in the kitchen. Instead I check my uni emails, which I don't do often enough. There's one from the course administrator. She asks how I'm doing and if I'm having any difficulties with the course. It's been noticed that I've been having problems with my assignments. Maybe I'd like to have a chat with my supervisor?

No, I would not. I've only failed two assignments. The first one was because I didn't really try. The second one was because they took off marks for late submission. How was I supposed to spot that in the pages and pages of submission guidelines? Besides, we aced the presentation. I'm not doing *that* badly.

I send a polite reply and decide to make a start on being a good student. Uni is definitely harder than school; I need to stop coasting. I get my books out, open the lecture slides and try to concentrate.

I don't get as much done as I'd hoped. It's soon time to head out and referee the Under Fourteens match. That at least is fun. I'm in charge and the kids have to do what I say, even if they bad-mouth me half the time. It's a pity the play isn't better. It's all route one, with one goalie kicking the ball up the field and the other booting it back. Every now and then players take each other out with some really lousy tackles. It gets me running up and down the pitch, though, before I settle down to more uni work back at halls.

The place is still pretty empty and I wonder what everyone else is up to. I pick up my phone and check out what everyone is doing online. There's football, football, guys getting drunk, computer games, more football. Lily's posted a series of ballroom dance pics. Yet another new hobby?

As I continue scrolling down, a reply appears from Gemma Anderson. She includes a picture in response to Lily's. A Jack Vettriano painting of dancers on the beach, with the comment: **You soon?** Lily's response is instant: **Me never. And shouldn't you be** ... She adds a gif of a girl playing a grand piano.

How's Gemma managing to practise for her audition as well as her Grade Eight? Which reminds me, I should probably be thinking about piano practice myself, if I'm actually going to sit this exam. I do the next best thing and send Gemma a direct message.

Jamie: How's the practising going?

There's a long pause. While I wait, I open tabs on my computer with all the coursework I've still got to do. I put them neatly in order, most urgent first. My phone vibrates.

Gemma: OK I think. You?

I snort, remembering the Shostakovich. Honestly? I reply:

Jamie: Bad! And non-existent now I'm back at uni. No piano.

Another pause, shorter this time.

Gemma: That's a shame. Can't you use one in the music department?

I hadn't thought of that. The university is so big I'd forgotten there even was a Music department.

Jamie: I think they're for music students only.

Gemma: You should go and ask. If they know you're doing Grade 8 they'll realise you're serious about your music.

Yeah, maybe.

I appreciate the encouragement, but I don't think I *am* serious about my music. At least, not about piano. That was always more Mum's thing. I like singing. That's what I do for myself: sing and play guitar.

Gemma has gone offline. I try to do some studying, but get lost down the black hole of reading about banking crises on Wikipedia. Before I know it, it's after midnight. Too late to do any proper work now. Instead I get down my guitar off the top of the wardrobe. I know I'll disturb half the people in the flat if I play now, but what the hell, they disturb me often enough.

Gemma

I just had a conversation with Jamie Abernethy. Not a real conversation, obviously, just a few messages. But I think Saturday was the first time I'd ever said much more than "Hi" to him, and we've definitely never messaged each other.

It must be difficult for him, being away at uni and so busy, and having this piano exam to deal with. I hope he manages to find somewhere to practise. He was pretty rusty when I heard him at Mrs Marshall's. Or maybe he was just a bit shaken after the car skidded off the road. I would have been. It was bad enough just driving with Mum beside me.

On Monday morning I get up early. I let Toby, our ancient collie-cross, out and then do some piano practice. I love playing. It takes me to another place, where there's just me and the music and I don't have to worry about anything.

That's when I'm playing alone. When I play in

front of an audience it's completely different. Then, I can't hear the music over the voices in my head saying *Everyone is looking!* And *You're so useless!* And *You'd better not throw up.* I don't know how Lily does it, speaking in public, doing all her head girl stuff without batting an eyelid. She even enjoys it.

I'm late for school but that's nothing unusual. And it does have the advantage that no one (i.e. Lily) can ask me again if I've decided what to do about the Conservatoire audition. I have a driving lesson straight after school, which doesn't go too badly. Pattie McNaught, my instructor, is always calm even though her job must be terrifying, and I think now I've got over my first nine months' nerves I'm getting the hang of things. She drops me off at Mrs Marshall's to do yet more preparation for the audition I still haven't agreed to.

'Excellent,' says Mrs Marshall after I play the Bach right through for the third time. 'Beautiful timing, really good emotion. You are coming on, Gemma.'

'Thanks,' I say shortly. All the positive reinforcement makes me even more nervous.

She fixes her piercing gaze on me. 'I was wondering if you could do me a favour.' It's the look you get when she's asking whether you've practised your arpeggios and she already knows you haven't. But this time I haven't done anything wrong. I don't think.

'Yes?'

'You know I've said before that teaching piano seems to be either feast or famine? Too many pupils half the time, not enough the other.'

I nod doubtfully. I don't remember that. Why would I?

'I've had a sudden influx of requests for lessons from new learners. I don't like to turn them down, but I'm struggling to fit them all in. I wondered if you would take on one or two for me.'

'Me?' I hope I sound as appalled as I feel.

'I think you'd be excellent, Gemma. Mrs Guthrie told me how good you are with new singers in the school choir. She said you get a lot out of them, without being in the least bossy.'

I look down at the piano, wishing I'd never started helping out with the choir. At the time it had seemed the perfect way to avoid doing any solos myself.

'I don't do much.'

'I've got a couple of little girls who I thought would be perfect for you. One in particular, because she only lives a couple of streets away from your house.'

'I don't really think ...'

'You'd be doing me a real favour, Gemma. And, of course, you'd be paid for your work.'

I'm wracking my brains trying to think of a way of getting out of this, but she seems to think that the mention of money will convince me. And of course, it would be amazing to have some extra cash. But teaching? No way!

'Consider it, Gemma. You can just start with the one,' says Mrs Marshall happily, 'and then see how it goes. I'll give Rosie's mum your phone number and she can arrange a time with you.'

'I—'

'Now let me hear your technical piece one more time.'

Automatically I change the sheet music and start playing. Playing is easier than talking. She can't really think I'm considering this teaching thing, can she?

As I leave, Mrs Marshall hands me a bundle of books. 'These are the ones I use for brand new learners. I have a few spare copies so you're welcome to borrow them.'

Apparently she doesn't just think I'm considering it. She thinks I've already agreed.

Gemma

A message comes up on my phone:

Jamie: You decided about the audition yet?

I'm already scowling in annoyance when I realise the message isn't from Lily, or Sarah, or Donny. It's from Jamie.

We've chatted online a couple of times now about the Grade Eight exam, and I hadn't been able to help mentioning the stupid audition.

I find myself typing.

Gemma: I think I might do it. I know I'll be crazy nervous though.

I'm thinking that the audition is in Glasgow, Jamie is in Glasgow ... Not that I'd see him while I was there, of course.

Jamie: You'll be great. Aren't you the top music student at school?

Gemma: School's different. And I'm not top!

Jamie: I heard you are. But you're right about

school being different ...

I stare at the last message. It seems like an invitation to talk about something other than music, but why would Jamie Abernethy want to talk to me about *anything*? Unless he's missing Newton St Cuthbert?

I draft and redraft my reply.

Gemma: How's uni? As fun as you expected?

I hit send and wait anxiously. I check his updates online all the time, but asking directly feels daring.

Jamie: Not really.

Maybe he is homesick.

I suppose it must be difficult, juggling everything. Is the work really hard? I know I'd hate being away from home, on my own, but he doesn't need to hear that. Besides, I'm me and he's, well, *Jamie Abernethy*. Super-confident, super-capable ...

He messages back.

Jamie: It's fine.

Then, before I've had time to respond.

Jamie: Good luck with the audition.

He goes offline. I mean, I'm sure he's got better things to do. But I still spend ages wondering why he's been messaging me at all. I keep waiting for him to mention Lily, because that must be it: he still has feelings for her and I'm the approachable best friend. Then I'll have to find a way to say that Lily's really happy. Like, so much happier with Tom than she was with him.

That's the last thing Jamie needs to hear if he's already a bit down.

I wonder if there's anything I could do to cheer him up. And then I remember we hardly know each other and I'm the last person on earth you'd choose if you wanted to cheer someone up.

First thing the next morning I go on to the Conservatoire website, log in to my profile and accept the audition. Afterwards, I feel a bit sick, but at least it'll stop people getting on at me.

I tell Mum over breakfast. 'It's good you've made up your mind,' she says. 'And passing the audition still doesn't mean you have to accept the place they offer, you know. It doesn't commit you to anything.'

'I probably won't pass.'

'You'll be fine,' she says. She's not fussing and trying to boost my confidence like everyone else does. Maybe she knows that would just make me more nervous. Mum continues, 'Have you remembered you've got another driving lesson with Pattie after school? I'm hoping she's going to say any time now that you're ready to take your test. You've been having lessons for months.'

I mumble some kind of reply. Tom started learning at the same time as me and has already passed. Lily is talking about taking her test soon and she's only been learning for a couple of months. But they're them and I'm me. Personally, I think I need at least twenty more lessons.

It sort of helps, though, having the worry about driving to balance out the worry about the audition.

I don't see Lily all morning as we do different subjects. I'm sure the audition will be the first thing she asks about as we walk into town with Tom and Donny at lunchtime, so I pre-empt her. 'Anyone want to come up to Glasgow with me a week on Friday? I'd appreciate the company.'

'You've accepted!' Lily starts to leap around, overenthusiastic as ever, kissing me on both cheeks. 'That's brilliant,' she continues. 'We can leave after morning classes and head up together.'

'You can't *all* bunk off. We are prefects, you know.' I meant what I said: I really would appreciate some company. I just don't want this to turn into a big trip.

'It won't be bunking off,' says Lily happily. 'Donny and I have been saying for a while we want to go up again and have a proper look around the Drama department before our auditions. I'm sure we'll get permission for that. And Tom's such a top student, no one's going to object to him having a few hours off.'

'It'll be expensive if we all have to pay train fares,' I say, now wishing I'd kept quiet. This is starting to get stressful; I should just have asked Mum to go with me.

'So we'll go by car,' says Lily. 'Donny, would you be able to borrow your dad's?'

'I am not going if Donny is driving,' I say firmly. 'I've only been in the car with him once and his driving was worse than mine.'

Donny laughs. Good thing he's not easily offended.

'Aye,' says Lily, 'good point. Not sure any of us would survive a drive all the way to Glasgow with you, Donny. Maybe Tom can borrow his mum's car?' Lily nods like it's all sorted.

Tom slows his pace and says quietly to me, 'You know, if you don't want all of us trailing along, just say. Lily might be disappointed, but she'll listen if you insist.'

'It'll be okay,' I say doubtfully. At least if there's a crowd, I'll be able to slide into the background. It might even distract me from worrying too much about having to perform. Unlikely, but it might.

Gemma

The trip to Glasgow turns into one of Lily's events. After I get over my initial doubts, I don't really mind. It means I don't have to worry about travel arrangements ('logistics', as Lily calls it) and don't even have much chance to stress about the audition itself. There's too much going on.

Lily's plan is that we have a very late lunch once we've got to Glasgow, and then she, Donny and I will go to the Conservatoire to look around while Tom meets up with someone he knows who's doing Engineering at Strathclyde. It's one of his university options for next year.

As Lily, Donny and I make our way along Sauchiehall Street, I reach for my hair to chew the end of it. Then I remember that Mum (supported by Lily) has made me put it up in a stupid bun. What am I supposed to chew on now? I try the nail of my little finger but Lily swats it away.

'I thought you'd stopped biting your nails, like, decades ago?'

'I need something to distract me.' I pat my hair, wondering if I can pull down a tendril.

Donny takes hold of that hand. 'No way. You are not messing up that glorious hair. Come along, let's sing as we go, that'll distract you! How about we start with that Ed Sheeran and Beyoncé duet, 'Perfect'? Because that's what your performance is going to be. I'll do Ed's part.' He tries to make a start but even Lily is appalled at the idea of making such a spectacle of ourselves.

'Calm down Donny. Just because you're going to see Ricky later.'

'Exactly. So how can I calm down?' Donny flaps a hand in front of his face, as though he's too hot.

After the audition we're meeting up with Donny's new boyfriend, Ricky. Well, new-ish. They've apparently been seeing each other in Glasgow for a few months, but it was only a couple of weeks ago that the rest of us got to meet him for the first time. I hardly spoke to him. I was a bit intimidated, to be honest. He's big; tall and well built, with dark eyes and dark hair tied back in a ponytail. Plus he's studying Maths. Who would voluntarily study Maths?

But Donny *really* seems to like him, so I suppose that's the main thing. It's the first time he's ever introduced us to a boyfriend.

All the while I'm wondering if I've got the right music with me, if we've come at the right time, if I can remember even the first word of my first song …

Before I know it, we're at the Conservatoire; a brick-built block of a building up one of the side streets.

'You've still got half an hour,' says Lily. 'Come with us to the Drama department?'

'No.' They've been good and supportive and distracting. But now I need to be on my own. 'The instructions said there's a side room where you can warm up. I'm going to go and get ready.'

They both look like they want to hug me, but I think any more emotion might push me right over the edge. I hurry away with a little backward wave.

I'm halfway down a corridor when I realise I don't actually know where I'm going. There'd been one sign that said *MUSIC AUDITIONS*, which is why I came this way, but now there's nothing. Not even anyone to ask. The corridor has a really high ceiling and an echoey tiled floor. I'm wearing shoes with heels to make me seem taller, and they're making a horrible clickety noise.

This was a huge mistake. I should just turn around and walk right back out.

A woman comes around the corner ahead of me with a clipboard in her hand. 'Hello there! You must be here for the Music audition, which means you're either Gemma or Susan.'

'Gemma,' I whisper.

40

'Excellent. In plenty of time to do some warm-up practice. Come this way.'

She doesn't actually grab hold of my arm, but it feels like it. There's no escape now.

Jamie

Fourth assignment of the semester back; third one failed. I would have failed even if I hadn't got points deducted for submitting late. Again. And it wasn't even difficult, according to my classmates. I just hadn't been able to find the time to make sense of it. I'm surprised I even got thirty-five percent.

It's a new experience, failing at things. I've never been a straight-A student like my brother Michael, but I've always done well enough. There were loads of people who did worse at school, so I felt like I was one of the bright ones. Big fish in a small pond and all that. Now I'm on a course where everyone is as bright as me – make that brighter, apparently. It really is time to get my act together. I'm sure once I start making a real effort it'll be fine.

'Coming to the Union to celebrate another assignment down?' says Innis as we file out of our lecture.

He and the rest probably are celebrating, but I'm happy just to drown my sorrows. And it is Friday. Why not take the evening off and start again tomorrow?

'Aye, why not?'

The Union is a cavernous building, not much to look at from the outside and even more of a dive within. We like it anyway. At this time on a Friday afternoon it's quiet. We have a beer, and when someone suggests another, I stand everyone a round. I've just got paid for some refereeing and it makes them stay around a while longer.

'Cheers, mate,' says Kris as I hand him his pint. 'And where do you stand on the Man City – Chelsea thing? Who do you think's gonnae win the league?'

'Too early in the season to say,' I reply. 'Why are you talking about English football anyway?' Football is something I can talk about for weeks on end. But why do people always have to go for the big teams? And the big *English* teams?

'Rather them than bloody Dundee that you're such a fan of.'

'Dundee United,' I say automatically.

'It's no' even like it's your local team. Why don't you support Queen of the South?'

'Because I don't live in Dumfries?'

'Still your nearest team.'

'They're my second team.' Everyone's allowed two teams, right? My dad's from Dundee and he's always been a mad Dundee United fan.

Innis waves his half-empty glass. 'If you're allowed two teams, then Barcelona has to be one of them. They're the only ones who play the game like it should be played ...'

I take another long pull of my beer and let the banter wash over me. When I start paying attention again, everyone's moved on to talking about their courses, which is harder to bask in.

'Thought it might be a bit of a jump moving on to uni, but it's been alright so far.' Innis takes a satisfied swallow of his beer.

'It's really no' so bad, is it?' Kris nods. 'I might even join the Economics Society. It's kind of interesting knowing how these things work.'

'Might come along with you,' says one of the other guys.

Are they mad? Are they honestly saying they're finding this course interesting? That they'd voluntarily attend meetings to talk about *economics*?

I offer to get another round in. Anything so I don't have to contribute to this discussion.

Gemma

The audition is a disaster. Halfway through my main piano piece I get distracted and start wondering what the interviewers might be writing. I play on autopilot for what feels like forever. Once my attention snaps back, I've no idea if I even played the right thing, let alone if I played it well. In the singing my voice was shaking on the high notes. They'll definitely have noticed that, not to mention me dropping the sheet music during the sight-reading part. They must be feeling sorry for me, as they let me do the final piece.

'Don't ask,' I say when I meet up with Lily and Donny on the steps outside. I knew I wasn't going to pass – I didn't even want to – but God I feel like an idiot!

'It probably wasn't–'

'I don't want to talk about it.' It's so unusual to hear me raising my voice that even Lily gives in.

'Well, at least it's over now. Come on, we're meeting Ricky down here.'

I'm still shaking. I don't object when Lily hooks her arm through mine and draws me along. If she weren't holding me up, I might just collapse right there.

We meet up with Ricky and a short while later Tom appears. They discuss what to do next and I huddle inside my smart black coat. I can hear what they're saying, I just can't be bothered to work out what the words mean.

When Lily takes my arm again and says, 'Okay, Ricky says the Student Union is this way,' I let her pull me along again. It's only when we climb a very steep street and troop inside a scruffy, modern building that I start to take notice.

'Where are we?'

'Student Union.' She waves at a sign that looks like graffiti except that it's framed. 'Duh.'

'But we're not students.'

'No, but Ricky is. He's going to show us around.'

'Don't you have to be eighteen …' I start off, doubtfully, but nobody seems to share my worries. I suppose I don't have to have an alcoholic drink – even if I could probably do with one right now.

'I'll get the drinks,' says Ricky. 'They might not serve you lot.'

We give him our orders and some money. I ask for a coke but Lily persuades me to order something stronger. I pull a face as the unfamiliar heat hits the back of my throat. Lily shrugs unapologetically. 'At least you don't look like you're about to faint anymore.'

She's got a point. I settle into a corner, sipping my vodka and coke and looking about. It's interesting to see what a Student Union is like. It's basically like a badly decorated pub, with a sticky floor and stained tables – and lots and lots of young people around. Most of them seem to be fairly drunk already, although it's still only late afternoon. Drunkest of all is Jamie Abernethy.

I don't know why I didn't see or hear him before. He's with the loudest crowd, and he's probably the noisiest of them. This is odd. I've never seen Jamie this rowdy before.

Lily follows my line of sight. 'What's he doing here?'

'Doesn't he go to uni here?' I say, like I don't already know.

'So he should be studying at this time of day, not getting plastered.'

'It's going to be such a laugh being a student,' says Donny. He squeezes Ricky's leg happily.

'He's coming over,' I say, because Jamie has spotted us. I want to hunch down in my seat and disappear. I'm not sure he's ever seen Lily and Tom together before. What if it's awkward?

'Hiya!' he says brightly, swaying. 'What're youse all doing here?' He must be really drunk if he's talking like that. 'Hey, Gemma, was it your audition?'

Lily and Donny turn to stare at me, clearly wondering how on earth Jamie would know about my audition. I nod, keeping my eyes on the table.

'How'd it go? Bet you killed it.'

I wait, but when no one else seems inclined to answer for me, I mutter, 'Not great.'

'She's not talking about it,' says Lily, taking pity on me. 'But we're sure she was brilliant.'

'I wasn't.'

'I'm sure you were,' says Jamie. When I glance up, I'm surprised to see he's looking at me, not at Lily. 'Go for it. Glasgow's a great place, you know?'

There's a bit more disjointed conversation then, thank goodness, he wanders off. I glance at Tom, but he doesn't seem put out about seeing his girlfriend's ex, and Lily has gone back to cross-questioning Ricky about where the best nightclubs are. I'm the only one who watches Jamie as he meanders back across the room. Is he going to carry on drinking?

I get my answer when one of his friends comes back from the bar with a tray of four pints and some shots. Can't they see he's had enough?

It's like watching car-crash TV. Jamie tries to sit on a stool and almost falls off. Then someone turns up the music and he jumps up and starts throwing himself about, not even slightly in time to the beat. No one else is dancing.

I nudge Lily so that I can slide out of my seat. Someone needs to stop Jamie making a complete fool of himself.

Before I've even stood up, Jamie catches his foot on a chair leg and goes flying. He lands with a crash on the grimy floor.

I say, 'We've got to help him.'

Lily watches with interest rather than concern. 'I'm sure his friends'll help him.'

I'm not even sure they are his friends. One is on his phone and the other two are laughing hysterically, making no move to help. Jamie has got to his knees, but that seems to be all he can manage.

'Come on yer numpty,' someone shouts. 'Cannae hold your drink or what?'

Jamie just stays there, kneeling, head lolling.

I push Lily. 'Come on! We've got to do something.'

She sighs and then nods and follows me.

'You okay, Jamie?' I say, bending down to his level.

'Fine,' he slurs. 'Just gimme a minute.'

'He's going to be sick,' says Tom, who has joined us.

'He can't be sick in here,' says one of his so-called friends. 'We'll be fined for the clean-up. Or banned. Fucking nightmare.'

'Let's get him outside then,' says Lily. She takes one arm and nods at Tom to take the other. They're both way taller and stronger than me. They heave and Jamie staggers to his feet.

'Come on,' says Lily.

'Better take him back to his room,' says the same friend as before. He gives us the name of the student hall but doesn't offer to show us the way.

Tom nudges Jamie and they begin to make their way across the room like some ungainly, six-legged creature. We're on the first floor but somehow they get him down the stairs, helped by Donny and Ricky. We're out on the pavement when Jamie starts throwing up.

We all jump back, because – who wouldn't? It's disgusting. Jamie is left to balance himself with one hand against the wall, and the vomit just keeps on coming.

'He'll feel better after that,' says Donny approvingly.

I look in my bag and am pleased to find that I not only have a packet of clean tissues, I also have some anti-bacterial wipes. I get the wipes out and when Jamie seems to have finished, I edge closer and hold one out to him.

'Here.'

'What? Oh, thanks.' He wipes his mouth.

'Let's get out of here,' says Ricky.

He's right. People are staring and making wide detours around us.

'We'll walk back to your halls with you,' says Tom to Jamie. 'Come on, you lead the way.'

We all watch as he starts moving. He does, thank goodness, seem steadier on his feet. ''M'all right,' he says, 'don' need help.'

'We'll just go with you to make sure,' says Lily. I nod gratefully. We can't leave him like this.

Jamie heads towards the area where I know the uni halls are and we follow after him, none of us keen to get too close because, well, he's a bit smelly now. He drops the wipe in a bin and I pass him another, glad to be able to contribute something.

When we get to the door of the red-brick building Jamie gets out his key and pauses. 'I'm, er, fine now. Thanks.' But it's clear he isn't from the way the key wavers, missing the hole repeatedly.

Tom takes it from him and opens the door. 'I'll just see you inside,' he says with a sigh. 'The rest of you can wait for me here.'

I'm relieved. Jamie needs someone to make sure he's okay.

We stand around waiting for Tom to return, stamping our feet and rubbing our hands to try and keep warm. The atmosphere is muted. Poor, poor Jamie.

On the plus side, no one is talking about my audition any more.

Jamie

Oh Jesus. Oh no. I've woken up lying fully clothed on my bed, with a disgusting taste in my mouth. Worst of all, I can remember who got me here. Lily and Tom Owen. And Gemma. Sweet, tidy, quiet Gemma, who'd handed me those wipes to help me clean up when …

I groan and reach for the glass of water by my bed. The glass of water Tom made sure I had before he left, as well as the bowl on the floor. I close my eyes. I can't think of anything more mortifying. Maybe I can slip back into unconsciousness and next time I wake this will all have been a dream. A nightmare.

My head is hurting so much there's no way I can get back to sleep. I don't know how long I lie there, with all these thoughts going around in my head. Why am I such an idiot? Why did the Galloway Academy crowd have to be there to see it? And why didn't any of my lousy uni friends offer a hand?

Eventually I sit up and the room spins and I think I'm going to be sick again. I'm not. I stagger to the tiny en suite. If I can just get out of these clothes and have a shower, maybe everything will be fine.

It's not exactly fine, but it is slightly better. I put on clean clothes, stuff the old ones in a bag until I can face thinking about them, and head to the kitchen. I need coffee, litres of it.

Innis is sitting at the table, tapping away at his laptop and spooning cereal into his mouth.

'Hey, you survived,' he says, grinning.

'Barely.' And no thanks to him.

'Yeah, you were really going some. Pity you faded so quick. We went on to that new club on West Street. Not bad.'

I grunt. Great for them. I make coffee (black because the milk is suspect) and head back to my room. I've got the whole weekend ahead of me and for once I'm not going to waste it. I'm really going to sort myself out.

I clean my room, put a wash on and make a start on all the work I need to catch up with. Gemma messages me to ask if I'm feeling okay. I can't think of anything witty to say after last night, so I just say I'm fine and leave it at that.

Gemma

I feel so bad about seeing Jamie in such a mess, and us all having to just leave him, that I don't do any more post-audition stressing. What does it matter if I made a fool of myself and failed? I've lost nothing I wanted.

What I'm concerned about is that we made things worse for Jamie, with us lot being there. It must have been embarrassing for him. Maybe that's why he hardly responded to my message. Though I didn't think much of those friends of his. They thought the whole thing was a joke. People can die from drinking too much. I've looked it up. I know.

And then Monday afternoon is here and I'm due to give my first piano lesson to this girl Rosie. I *really* don't want to do it.

'So why did you agree?' asks Lily, who's walking home with me so she can see Sarah.

'I didn't agree. Mrs Marshall just took it for granted.'

'You know, Gemma, you need to stand up for yourself more.'

I shrug. That's easy for her to say. I notice she doesn't think it when I stand up to her.

I reach for my ponytail. 'I really don't like kids. My aunt's always trying to get me to look after my cousins and they just, like, scream and cry for no reason at all.'

'They're kind of wee, aren't they? This Rosie shouldn't scream and cry. Didn't you say she's ten?'

'I don't think that guarantees anything,' I say gloomily.

'It's not all bad. You get paid.'

I just nod.

I have precisely five minutes between getting home and the arrival of Rosie. If she's on time. I hate it when people aren't on time.

I dust the piano and lay out the books Mrs Marshall lent me. I've decided which one to start with, but first I'll need to explain the really basic things, like what the different notes are called. It's so long since I started learning that I can't remember my first piano lesson. I'm going in blind here. I should have asked Mrs Marshall for more advice …

The doorbell rings and I open it to a woman and a tall, thin girl. The girl is almost the same height as me, which stumps me a bit. I thought ten-year-olds were little.

'Come in,' I say, hardly above a whisper. I wish Mum was here to talk to Mrs Thomson, but she's not back from work.

I lead them through to the room Dad built on at the back of the garage so I can practise my music without driving everyone else mad. I put the heater on in here when I got home but it's still cold.

'Rosie and I'll be working in here,' I say.

'Sorry?'

Oh why can't I have a loud voice like Lily? I try again. 'Rosie and I will be working on the piano in here. There's a seat there, if you want, or you can sit in the lounge. I think Mum has some magazines you could read ...' I'm babbling now.

Mrs Thomson nods, 'I'll go and sit in the lounge. Other days I won't stay, but I thought I should be here the first time.'

I nod. Maybe there won't be other days. Maybe I'll be absolutely useless and they'll never come back.

She heads to the lounge and I gesture to Rosie to sit down on the piano stool. I take a deep breath. She's here now so I've got to do my best. And to be honest, she looks almost as nervous as I feel.

I've brought out the two-person stool so that I can sit down next to her.

'The most important thing is that you should enjoy your piano playing.' I'd thought about this last night and I'm really glad I remembered to say it. 'Piano can be – is – fun. You'll need to learn the keys, and how to read music, and practise, but I want you to have fun, too. Okay?'

The girl nods her head and her dark, curly hair bounces.

I play a little tune one-handed, just something to make her smile. I feel sorry for her. I know what it's like to be frozen with nerves.

Then I show her how to find middle C. I place my thumb on the key and play it in time while I sing 'I am C, mi-ddle C', a few times. Then I shift to make space for her. 'Your turn.'

She bites her lip and puts her thumb on the note and presses it. The sound it makes seems to surprise her.

'Go on. Do it again.'

She presses it a few more times, each one growing louder.

'Brilliant. Now, play it as we sing along together. Are you ready? I am C! Mi-ddle C!'

She does it four or five times, singing and banging louder on each occasion. When she stops, she's giggling. It's quiet, but it's an improvement.

'Right, now we'll move on to the other notes. C is the one to the left of every set of two black keys, see? And then you have D here, and E ...'

I can do this. I don't know whether it's Rosie's quiet concentration, or just the sound of the piano notes that soothes me, but the lesson isn't nearly as bad as I'd expected. I want Rosie to learn and she seems to want it too. At this stage, the stuff we're doing is so easy there's no way she can get it wrong. She might not know a huge amount at the end of her forty-five minutes, but she's almost smiling and seems happy to take the book I give her with a few basic exercises. And she definitely knows where middle C is!

Her mum pays me the fee, which fortunately Mrs Marshall had already agreed, and when they leave I dance around the room. I did it! I was probably a bit slow and boring, but I got all the way through to the end of the lesson without getting tongue-tied. I got paid. And Mrs Thomson asked Rosie if she wanted to come back, which she did, so I'm giving her another lesson next week.

And I'm actually okay with it. Maybe Lily is right and it is a good thing to challenge yourself sometimes.

Gemma

On the second Friday in December I get a response from the Conservatoire. I stare at my phone in horror. I've tried not to think about that embarrassing audition. I was convinced there was no way I would get in. But can you believe it? They've offered me a place.

I'm really annoyed! Couldn't they see it wasn't right for me? Plus deciding whether to audition was hard enough. Now I have to decide whether to accept a place or not. I really don't want to go. But what if I turn it down and then have second thoughts?

I hate making decisions!

We're sitting in the Sixth Form common room. I'm with Lily and Donny. I realise there were pings from Lily and Donny's phones too. Does that mean the Conservatoire is sending out all its decisions now?

Lily is looking dismayed. 'Lil?' I say. She and Donny were the ones who were dead certs to get in. *I* was the question mark.

'Wey hey!' shouts Donny, getting up and doing a dance around the room, which mostly involves tripping over bean bags and feet. 'I'm in, I'm in, I'm in!'

'Lily?' I repeat.

She drops her phone onto her lap. 'It's a no for me.' She speaks calmly and if you didn't know her well, you wouldn't hear the slight wobble in her voice.

'That's crazy. Why wouldn't they take you?'

She sighs. 'My acting was okay, I think. But it's not just about acting, is it? They try you out for singing and dancing as well. They're looking for all-round skills. Obviously I don't have what it takes.'

'They're being ridiculous,' I say, furious with the stupid college for being wrong about both of us. 'Honestly. Their loss. They clearly have no idea what they're missing.'

She gives me a small smile and then shouts over to Donny, 'Congrats to you, mate. You're going to be a star!'

To his credit, Donny stops capering around and comes to sit down again. 'And you?'

'The Conservatoire has declined the pleasure of my attendance. But no problem, I quite fancied that Politics and Philosophy course in Dundee. Or Politics and Sociology in Edinburgh.'

'I'm sorry,' says Donny, looking like he really is. 'I don't understand. They must be mad. Why would they take me and not you?'

'Because you're better?' suggests Lily.

She gets up suddenly and waves to someone who has just come in. It's Tom. He waits for Lily by the door and after they've exchanged a few words they head back out together, his arm around her shoulders.

'It's great the Conservatoire lets people know so early,' says Donny, back to being happy.

Stupidly, I nod. Which seems to remind him that I also applied. He leans forwards, trying to see my phone screen. 'You heard anything?'

'Aye.'

'And?'

I drop the phone beside me and let out a huge whoosh of a sigh. 'I got accepted too. What on earth am I going to do now?'

Jamie

Despite all my good intentions in November, I'm not getting on so well with studying. I'm really trying. I restrict my drinking to weekends. Unless I'm refereeing, I spend the weekday evenings in my room sitting at my desk. The trouble is, it's all so boring. I read it, but it all seems meaningless. Still, the longer I do this, the more chance there is that some of it will stick. I think of all the recognition I used to get at school. That's never going to happen here. Even if I start doing better, I'm never going to be amazing here. But I have to keep trying.

I've stayed off social media for a while, so as not to get distracted. But with the Christmas holidays approaching, I eventually give in. Donny Miller has got into the Conservatoire to do Drama, which means Gemma will probably have heard whether she's got a place to do Music. We haven't been in touch since the day following that drinking fiasco. No reason why we should be. But I really want to know whether she's got a place or not, and there's nothing about it online.

I message her.

Jamie: I see the Conservatoire offers are out. You heard anything?

It doesn't take her long to reply.

Gemma: Yes. I heard this morning.

Jamie: And?

Gemma: They've offered me a place.

Jamie: Knew they would! Congrats.

I'm really pleased for her. I don't know why she hasn't got more confidence in herself. Maybe this will be the boost she needs.

There's a longer wait until her next message.

Gemma: Actually I'm not sure I'll take it.

I stare at the screen. Everyone with any talent in music or drama is desperate to get into the Conservatoire. To get offered a place and then turn it down? Unheard of.

Another message comes through before I've thought how to answer.

Gemma: Lily didn't get in.

I consider that. I'm surprised because whatever Lily does she seems to succeed at. But I don't feel too sorry for her. She'll be fine whatever. I hope Gemma realises that.

Jamie: Shame about Lily. But that's not why you're thinking of not accepting is it?

Gemma: No, it's not that.

Jamie: So, why?

I realise I really am interested in how Gemma thinks, what's going on behind that quiet exterior. I wait to see what she'll come back with.

Gemma: I'm not really sure it's what I want to do.

Jamie: But you decided to go for the audition. I thought that meant you were keen?

Gemma: I went for the audition because everyone kept telling me to, and I didn't think I'd get in.

That makes me grin. There's something funny – and interesting – about Gemma.

Jamie: Hey, you shouldn't do things just because people expect them of you.

Gemma: That's easy for you to say.

What does that mean? Does she seriously think I don't have expectations, millions of them, weighing down on me too? She has no idea. But this isn't about me.

Jamie: No need to decide straight away.

Gemma: I know. Thanks.

Jamie: Might be an idea to come and have another look around, see a bit more of Glasgow?

Gemma: Maybe I'll do that.

I hesitate, thumbs hovering over the screen. I think this might actually have been why I made the suggestion. But last time she saw me I was acting like a drunken idiot. I can't think why she'd want to see me again, but …

Jamie: If you do come up, give me a shout. Maybe we can have coffee or something.

There's a very long pause after that, and then a one-word reply.

Gemma: Thanks.

Clearly that was not a welcome suggestion.

Gemma

The Christmas break was a great distraction, only slightly marred by having my Grade Eight exam on the first Monday. The concert with the Carlisle Junior Orchestra was fun, and I think we saw every single member of Mum and Dad's extended families between Christmas and New Year. Meaning loads of presents, and lots and lots of cake. Lily and Donny arranged a couple of get-togethers for the school crowd, too, involving alcohol rather than cake. They were fun too, in a different way.

Now it's the new term and it's time to make a decision. I've been looking through the Conservatoire website, watching all these videos of people jumping about and laughing and performing like they're born to it. Everyone happy and loud and confident. Lily would have been in her element there. I hope she's not too disappointed about not getting in. Although, I don't think I ever saw her as a career actress. She's more suited to leading a country. Or possibly the world.

I'm much less sure about me.

The idea of accepting makes me feel nervous and sick every time I try to think about it. I do love music, it's true, but it's always been something I do for me. I hate performing. There's no way I can avoid that if I'm studying at the Conservatoire. I've more or less decided to decline the offer, but Jamie has been so encouraging the couple of times we've messaged each other since. Positive, but not trying to convince me to decide one way or the other. And he's suggested *twice* that I go up and have a look around Glasgow again. Maybe I should. I've been nervous at the thought of leaving home (along with the whole performing thing) but that day we all went up to Glasgow wasn't too bad. It's a big city, true, but it's got a friendly feel to it.

I chew the end of a length of hair and then toss it back in disgust. I really need to stop doing that.

Maybe I will go up to Glasgow again, but by myself. I can't make a decision when everyone's around. They're my friends, and I'm really lucky to have them. But it's hard to concentrate on what I want with all their opinions weighing in. If I go up on my own, I'll be able to get a clearer idea of what it would be like living there.

And, of course, I might get to see Jamie. It's really kind of him to offer to meet up. I hope he's not regretting it. I'm not sure I've got the nerve to message him to make arrangements just in case he is.

Maybe the best thing is just to put the whole idea

aside for a few days until I have the time to think about it properly.

I give Rosie another lesson, which seems to go okay. I cancel my next lesson with Mrs Marshall. What do I need more lessons for now? She'll just nag me about making a decision and possibly inflict another pupil on me. Then I go round to see Sarah.

That is one useful thing I can do. I chivvy her along with her National Five studies. And Sarah definitely needs the encouragement. She was doing so well in the autumn. There was even talk of her going back to school this term, but it hasn't quite worked out. If she does too much, she still has to spend the next day or three in bed. I remind her that she's still loads better than she was this time last year, when they thought her chronic fatigue might never improve. She nods, but doesn't look convinced.

She says, 'And how about you? You decided yet whether you're going to take up the Conservatoire offer?'

'Has Tom decided where he's going to study yet?' Diversion is usually a good tactic, as I've learned over the years with Lily. Tom's results are so good he's already had unconditional offers from at least four universities.

Unfortunately, diversion doesn't always work. Sarah nods. 'Aye. He's accepted the offer from Edinburgh. So, what have you decided?'

I sidestep again. 'But I think now Lily's not going

to the Conservatoire her first choice will be Dundee. I thought Tom was sure to go there too.'

'Why? Just because they happen to be going out, that doesn't mean they need to be in the same city. They should do what's best for them. It's not like Edinburgh is far from Dundee, is it? And if you're in Glasgow you won't be far from either of them.'

I feel like *she's* trying to make *me* feel better. That was not my plan when I came over.

'Lily not getting into the Conservatoire has nothing to do with whether I decide to go or not.'

Sarah just raises her eyebrows, which is really annoying. Does everyone think that's why I'm dithering? Honestly, does no one know me at all?

I sigh. 'Donny's going, so it's not as though I wouldn't know anyone.'

'That's true. So why are you still undecided?'

'Because I'm not sure what to do! I don't know how everyone can be so sure about everything. It's not like they know how they're going to feel next week, never mind next year. What if I hate it?'

'What if you don't?'

'Sarah, you're not helping.'

She shrugs then and laughs. 'But you've cheered me up. That was the reason you came over, wasn't it? To cheer up poor Sarah? So you've succeeded in that, at least.'

'If poor Sarah's feeling so energetic, maybe she should get on with her studies?'

Jamie

I head back to uni straight after New Year. I still haven't plucked up the courage to tell Mum and Dad I've got two re-sits. They were so appalled with the marks I *did* tell them about, I decided to omit that I'd failed Economics and Accounting completely. Which probably wasn't helped by my missing one or two lectures. They were just so dull.

Mum and Dad pretended to put my grades down to adjusting to the social life of first year. Everyone finds it hard to find the right balance, they said, but I know what they were thinking: *Your brother never struggled.*

Bloody perfect Michael.

Innis is back too. These days I'm not so sure having someone in my flat doing the same course is such a good thing after all. He wants to compare marks and discuss subject choices for this semester.

I say, 'Haven't quite decided yet. I need to head off, got a five-a-side match.'

'To be honest mate, I don't know how you find the bloody time to be a referee along with everything else.'

Nor do I. Or, rather, I *don't* have the time. I just do it anyway, because it's the one thing I'm really enjoying about my life right now. I think I'm pretty good at it too, which helps.

On the first day of lectures, when I'm trying to pretend everything is fine, I get an email from my supervisor saying he wants to see me and will I call by his office this afternoon. This isn't a polite "How are you getting on?" from the administrator. It's a direct instruction.

Not good.

I almost decide not to go anyway. He'll bawl me out for my work and tell me to pull myself together – stuff I know already. It's just that it's not so easy to do, even when you completely get that you have to. I am trying, I really am. I don't know why this year has turned out to be so hard. I'd been so looking forward to getting away from home, not having Mum monitoring my every move. But I have to admit, now that I'm here – well, things aren't quite as easy as I'd thought they'd be.

What if my supervisor tries to throw me off the course? He can't do that, can he?

I suppose I'd better go along and find out.

At two o'clock I head to the admin building. I don't say anything to Innis or the others. They might sympathise or they might laugh and I can't cope with either.

My supervisor is an old guy called Graham on the verge of retirement. He waffles a lot in lectures but he seems well meaning. I've never spoken to him one-to-one before.

'Afternoon, afternoon. Take a seat.' He moves a pile of papers so that I can sit down. He looks at me over the top of his glasses, and then at the screen of his computer, like he's forgotten what he summoned me for. 'Er, yes. Jamie Abernethy, isn't it?'

'Yes.'

'Well, Jamie. Your attendance record isn't great, and a couple of your tutors have raised concerns about your work. Yes, that's right. A few failed assignments, yes? And resits on two courses from the first semester?'

'Yes. But I'm settling down, starting to work properly now.'

He looks at me again. 'Everything, er, all right with you?'

What can you say to that? 'Yeah, fine.'

'You know, if you have any worries, financial or, er, emotional. Or if you feel this course isn't the right one for you. You know there are people you can talk to about these things?' He looks as uncomfortable with this conversation as I feel.

'No, there's no problem,' I say. There isn't. I can sort this. 'It's just taken me a bit of time to settle down. First time away from home and that.'

He nods gratefully. 'That's right. First year's never easy.'

It looks like I'm going to get away with this. I'm not being thrown off the course. Not yet, anyway. And he doesn't keep me long. He's not really interested, just going through the motions of checking up on me. There's probably some box he needs to tick.

I make my escape feeling weirdly disappointed. If things had come to a head, if he'd shouted and made a fuss, at least that would mean something had to happen. Now it looks like I'm just going to have to carry on.

I make my way to the talk we're having this afternoon. It's by one of the leading lights of Scottish business (their words). I think we're all supposed to aspire to be like him. Someone who wears a suit every day, writes reports, attends back-to-back meetings …

So *boring*.

I'm really starting to wonder if this is the life for me.

Gemma

I decide I will go to Glasgow. It might help me make a decision about what to do next year. I don't tell anyone but Mum, and I only tell her so that she'll give me a lift to the train in Dumfries.

'Lily and the others not going this time?'

'No.' I don't explain why I need to go alone and she doesn't ask. She's okay, my mum. A bit too chatty with strangers at times, but she doesn't push me to do stuff I don't want to do, or ask too many questions. Maybe it's because she's used to dealing with Dad. He's shy like me. I get my colouring from him too. Red hair, but not dark red. The kind of red that will go grey as soon as I turn thirty – thanks Dad!

I know I'm not much to look at and mostly I don't have a problem with that. I'm small and skinny and just kind of pale – even my freckles are faint. But today I've made more of an effort. I went through a make-up phase when I was about fourteen. It lasted two weeks.

But maybe mascara did make my eyes look a bit less … pale? Otherwise they're just a washed-out blue with sandy lashes. Faded like the rest of me.

So this morning I put on some mascara that Mum gave me ages ago. I'd only used it once then, and now the wand is quite dried up. I wonder if it can give me an eye infection? As I sit on the train watching the fields fly past, my eyes start to feel itchy. I'm definitely going to have to buy a new mascara if I'm going to carry on with this performance. Or maybe I'm allergic to make up? I wish I'd brought some wipes with me so I could take it off. Jamie will probably think I've made an effort just for him. Which I haven't. Not that I'm going to see him. I haven't messaged him in advance so he'll probably be busy.

The train seems to stop at about twenty stations before it gets to Glasgow, and at each one the sky is greyer and the rain heavier. The closer we get the more I think this was a bad idea. I'll get soaked and be freezing all day. I'll probably catch a cold. I know you don't actually catch colds from being cold but it does make you more susceptible. I've checked it out online.

Maybe I should just have a coffee at Central Station and get the next train back. I'll tell Mum it wasn't worth getting sick over. That I've already decided I really don't want to spend the next year away from home in Glasgow. I can go to uni in Dumfries, can't I? When I get home, I'm going to start looking into courses there. I don't want to use up my phone battery doing it now, just in case.

I sit and watch the buildings outside getting closer together and bigger and try to stop rubbing my eyes. It's just going to make them worse.

This whole trip was such a bad idea.

I walk across the plaza of Central Station to the wide exit. If it's still raining, I'll just get a coffee and go back home. If it's stopped, I'll walk up to the Conservatoire. Maybe.

And the rain has stopped! Which is really infuriating as it takes away my 'excuse' for going straight back home. With a huff, I zip up my coat and set off up the hill towards Sauchiehall Street.

I wasn't going to message Jamie in case he really was just being polite offering to meet up. But now I worry that if I don't tell him I'm here, I'm being rude. Finally I decide I'll send a very brief message, which he'll obviously reply to saying he's busy, if he replies at all, and that'll be fine. I won't have to worry about having hurt his feelings.

Gemma: In Glasgow now. Want to meet for a coffee? Don't worry if you're busy.

There.

Casual. Offhand. No big deal.

I stuff the phone in my pocket so that I can't keep checking to see if he's read the message. And after five minutes of wishing it were possible to *un*send a message, it vibrates.

Jamie: Of course! Just say where and when.

I stare at the screen for a while, just to make sure I'm processing it right. Jamie Abernethy wants to meet me. I mean, he's probably bored, or wants to catch up on news from home, or … I'm sure there are a million other possible reasons, but I don't have time to angst over them now. I remember there's a coffee place on the corner by the Conservatoire buildings. I suggest we meet there in half an hour.

It's started raining again. I hang around under the café awning until a figure comes walking swiftly along the pavement, a beanie pulled over his light brown hair, his face actually lighting up with a smile when he sees me.

Breathe, Gemma. I remind myself. *Just breathe.*

Jamie

Gemma's huddled against the rain in a black quilted coat that makes her look even tinier than usual. She's got the hood up, but when she sees me she pushes it back.

'Good,' she says a little breathlessly, 'now we can get inside. Is the weather always this bad in Glasgow?'

'At this time of year, at least,' I say. 'A real change from Galloway.'

She gives me a small smile to acknowledge the joke. We find a table and she starts extracting herself from the monster coat and unravelling a long rainbow coloured scarf. It makes me grin to watch her emerging from the cocoon. She's got her long hair tied back in a plait and her eyes are smudged with makeup.

We place our orders and then I say, 'So, have you looked around the college yet?'

'I had a quick look at the outside. I don't know if I'm allowed to go in.'

'How can you not be allowed to go in? They won't know whether you're a current student or not. Unless you have to use a student card to get access?'

'No, I don't think so. I didn't last time.'

'No problem then. I'll walk in with you afterwards.' She blushes, so I add quickly, 'But only if you want me to. I don't want to get in the way or anything.'

Gemma is so unlike Lily. With Lily you always knew what she wanted because she told you. With Gemma I've no idea if she's having a coffee with me because she felt obliged to, or because I'm the only person she knows in Glasgow.

'If you don't mind coming with me, that'd be good. But you've probably got loads of better things to do ...'

'Not this morning.' I'm glad that seems to be decided. 'So, how do you feel now you're in the big city again?'

'That it's cold. And grey. And big.'

'Aye, big cities tend to be big.'

She wrinkles her nose at me in a really cute way. 'But I find big kind of intimidating, you know? And then the Conservatoire itself – I've been looking at all the promo videos they've put up. It's all about teamwork and performing and getting yourself seen.' She pulls a face.

I remember her two performances in the talent show last summer. She'd been nervous then, but also really good. She'd probably have come first if I hadn't done that perennial crowd pleaser 'Caledonia', as insisted on by my mum. 'But you must have known all this about performing before you applied.'

She sighs. 'I suppose I did. But there's knowing and *knowing*. Putting in an application didn't feel real. I get so nervous before I perform that I feel sick. Why would I want to put myself through that over and over again? I enjoy playing piano for myself, and singing in groups, like a choir, but I really really *really* don't want to be a solo artist. And if I don't want that, maybe I should let the place at the Conservatoire go to someone who could make better use of it. Wouldn't I be being selfish if I took it when I know it's not what I really want to do?'

My eyes have been growing wider as Gemma speaks, partly because of how many questions she has and partly because I'm realising I should have asked more of my own when I was in her place. Once Mum realised I wasn't going to get the grades to do medicine like Dad and Michael, she'd steered me towards Accounting and Business Studies. I just kind of went along with it.

'It's good you're thinking it through in such detail,' I say, slightly bemused.

Gemma pulls around the end of her plait so she can nibble it, then tosses it back over her shoulder. 'Wouldn't it be nice to be sure?' she says, spreading her hands out and looking at them as though they might provide an answer. 'Wouldn't it be nice to know what you want to do and just go for it? That's what Donny and Tom are doing. And Lily knows the direction she wants to go in, if not the exact course.'

'Do you have any idea what you would want to study instead of Music?'

She sighs and drops her hands to the table. 'Not really.'

We're both quiet for a while, sipping our coffee. Gemma seems to have wound herself down, so I feel I need to make an effort.

'Didn't you go to the Junior Conservatoire or something?' I remember Mum trying to get me into that. It was held once a month in Glasgow for promising young musicians.

'No. I had the option of going, but I ended up doing the Junior Orchestra in Carlisle. That's where my gran lives so it was easier. And less scary. Like, even the words "Junior Conservatoire" are intimidating, aren't they?'

'More poncy than intimidating,' I say, which draws a weak smile.

'If I don't accept this place, I need to have another plan.' She taps her small fingers on the table. 'Otherwise my teachers will be going on at me to accept one of the other music courses.'

'Did you only apply for Music?'

'Aye. Stupid, right?'

'Not if that's all you're interested in.'

'It's all I'm good at. And I do like it, you know, but just for myself. I don't think I want to do it as a career.

81

I just don't know what I *do* want to do.'

I feel like saying join the club but, I remind myself, this isn't about me. Also, I don't need sympathy.

Gemma is fidgeting with the little packets of sugar. 'I should have looked into courses you can do in Dumfries. I'm sure that would have suited me better.'

'But what can you do in Dumfries?' I know they say there's a university there, but really it's just an offshoot of a couple of bigger ones. I've heard the courses are pretty limited.

'I know you can do Primary Teaching 'cause Mandy from your year is doing it. But I definitely don't want to do that.' She shudders.

I really feel for her, and even though I'm the last one who should be giving advice, I find myself saying: 'You know, sometimes the best thing is to take a gap year. See how you feel about things once you're out of school, and then make a decision.'

'You didn't take a gap year.'

'No.' It hadn't been an option for me. Mum doesn't believe in them, unless you're doing a round-the-world Raleigh Expedition or something else equally worthy that would look amazing on your CV.

'But what if I take a gap year and I still didn't know what I want to do with my life by the end of it? I'll have wasted a whole year and be no further forward.'

'I don't know if it counts as "wasting" a year.'

'It would for me. I'm not exactly one of those people that goes off to be a chalet girl in the Alps, or does bungee jumping in New Zealand, am I?' She looks serious and frustrated, but I can't help laughing. The idea of Gemma bungee jumping is actually quite funny.

She manages a small smile. 'See?'

'None of us really know what we can do until we try it.' God, why am I coming out with all these platitudes?

'Believe me, I am never ever going to try bungee jumping.'

After coffee we walk the short distance to the Conservatoire and Gemma says she'll go inside if I go with her, so I do. The entrance is massive and there are all these students sitting around in loud clothing, talking in loud voices. I don't say it, but it really doesn't seem like the kind of place Gemma would fit in.

Gemma says she'll think about it some more, but I'm guessing she's pretty much decided to decline. It's a shame, really. It would have been quite nice to have her in Glasgow next year. Assuming I manage to pass First Year and stay here myself.

I walk with her back to the station. We don't chat about much, but it's nice. Easy. And it feels good to be the guy who is helpful and supportive. Not the total git who gets drunk and is failing his course.

Jamie

When I first started refereeing, I hated the parents going on at me. New refs always get kids' matches because they're supposed to be easy. Believe me, they're not. Most of the kids are little shits and the parents are even worse. But if you survive that, you move on to older age groups. The good thing then is that there aren't usually any parents hanging around.

I must be doing something right because the Referee Association have given me quite a high-level game between two uni teams. Not my own uni of course, in case I'm be biased, but they're still guys about my age or older. They're not impressed when they see me.

'Allowing kids to ref now, are they?'

'Couldn't get any worse than that last wanker.'

'You watch their big centre forward, okay? Bastard dives.'

I call the captains over for the coin toss and give them the usual spiel about me being the ref and doing my job to the best of my ability but that they can help, too. They give me the briefest of nods without breaking their glare down. Great. Aggression from the get-go.

The first half isn't so bad. I speak to a couple of players about poor tackles, but I only have to give one yellow card for a clear foul. I don't know what their coaches said to them at half-time but clearly neither of them were willing to settle for a nil-nil draw. They come out raring to go and after ten minutes I've had to give three more yellow cards, there's been one near-fight, and the home team score from a free kick. Now the away captain is screaming at me.

'That was never a free kick! You're not quick enough! You need to keep up with the game!'

I blow the whistle and point to the centre for the restart.

'You just watch yourself after the game, right?' says the guy who puts the ball down. 'Only bloody losers take up reffing.'

'If your playing was half as good as my reffing, just think how good you'd be.'

He looks confused. 'Just remember, I'm watching you.'

Aye, it's really good when the threats begin. This time I ignore him and blow for the restart. He kicks towards one of the sidelines and the ball goes straight out of play.

Maybe I shouldn't smirk, but I can't help it. I might not be a brilliant player myself, but I don't think even I would kick the ball straight out from a restart. He swings towards me, arm slightly raised at my expression, then thinks better of it.

We jog down the pitch, me being really glad that the fitness training is one thing I've kept up with, and then the ball heads straight up the other end and I have to sprint after it. Another problem with these amateur games is there are no assistant refs so you need to see everything for yourself. I get there in time to see the big centre forward I'd been warned about jump for a cross and get hauled to the ground by his opponent. He yells in frustration. I blow and point for a penalty. Pandemonium breaks out.

The defender who pulled the guy down takes a swing at him as he tries to stand. The rest of his team are crowding round me, all shouting at once. One pushes me in the chest and when someone tries to pull him back, he turns around and punches him. I hold up my hand and blow the whistle again and again but no one's listening.

I might have been a bit scared for my own safety if I hadn't been raging. 'Both captains over here! Everyone else stand back.' I pull out the red card to send off the defender. Instead of dealing with his player, the captain starts screaming in my face, so close I can feel the spit spraying. I pull out a second red for him. Talk about the Laws of the Game. Both of them have broken half a dozen.

'You cannae send me off!' yells the captain, and tries to take a swing at me himself.

I take a step back but the other captain pushes the raised arm aside. 'He's only doing his job, yer numpty!' And now he's guilty of violent conduct.

I nearly have to abandon the game, but eventually we carry on with one team down to nine men and the other to ten. Five players have yellow cards.

At the end of the game they all start crowding round me again. The coaches join in.

'We're putting in an official complaint. Idiot ref!'

'You haven't heard the end of this!'

This is when it'd be nice to be reffing a professional game, where you have somewhere to go to get away from the players. Here we're all sharing the same open bit of field and even the few spectators are gathering round and shouting. I do the absolute minimum of rounding things off and barely pull on my jacket and tracksuit bottoms before I head for the train.

I need to get away. And I need to submit a match report, which isn't going to read well.

I don't think I did anything wrong. I could tell from the start there was history between the teams. I think back over it, not seeing what I could have done differently, and still feeling anxious. I suspect that that coach is right and this isn't the end of it.

It isn't. First thing the next morning I get an email from the Referees' Association. A complaint has been submitted against me via the Complaints Management

System. In the meantime, I'm being stood down and won't be asked to referee any games.

I'm almost too stunned to take it in. They can't suspend me!

I want to email them right back and tell them not to be so ridiculous. Then I decide I'd better check the handbook and I find that they're right about the rules. I go back and read their email again. Under no circumstances am I to contact the complainants. As if I would! I'll be invited to give my input in due course, should that be deemed necessary.

I'm helpless. It looks like that's the end of my refereeing career. Not that it was a career. It's more like volunteering, you get paid such a pittance. But at least I'd enjoyed it. And I'd thought I was good at it. Exactly how many things am I going to find out I suck at this year?

Gemma

'Just leave it now, Lily, okay?'

Lily's got the bright idea of listing all the pros and cons of me going to the Conservatoire, and going through them together.

'I'm just trying to be helpful,' she says.

'Maybe you're not actually, like, helping?' says Donny, who's sitting with us in the Sixth Form common room.

'It's a big decision for Gem to make. I thought it'd be good to have everything laid out.'

Thankfully the bell goes for the next lesson. I fold up Lily's extensive list and stick it in my bag. 'I'll think them over later.'

I head over to the Music department where I'm due to do composition with Mrs Guthrie. Normally I enjoy the sessions with her. There are only two students doing Advanced Higher Music so it's really informal. But at the end, when Lizzie is packing her bag to leave, Mrs Guthrie says, 'Have you got a couple of minutes, Gemma?'

I nod and supress a sigh.

Mrs Guthrie comes to lean against the front of her desk, much closer to me than I'd like. 'You know, Gemma, the whole school is very proud of you for getting this offer to study at the Conservatoire. Your Grade Eight marks were excellent, but this is really something special. It hardly ever happens to one of our pupils.'

'Donny Miller's got in to do Drama.'

'Well, Drama's a bit different, isn't it? In Music you're competing against not just the top singers and musicians in Scotland, but in the whole of the UK – of Europe even. Places there are very sought after.'

I nod, getting a sick feeling in my stomach.

'It's great to see all your hard work paying off,' says Mrs Guthrie, oblivious to my pain. 'I just wanted to say what a great example you are to the younger pupils.'

'Thanks,' I mutter.

'And here's something I'd like you to consider.' She picks up an A4 piece of paper. 'I know you weren't keen last year, but things are different now, aren't they?'

She hands the paper to me with a broad smile. If my heart could sink any lower, it would. It's about the Musicians Centre that opened in Central Scotland a few years ago. The paper Mrs Guthrie is waving in my face, forcing me to take, is about a week-long course for senior school pupils of "exceptional musical talent", the performers and teachers of the future. It's to allow them to work and socialise with professional musicians. There are practice rooms and a communal kitchen to "encourage dialogue".

None of which sounds any less horrific than it did last year. Why on earth does Mrs Guthrie think it will?

She stands up, pleased that she's got me to take the paper, and ushers me out before I have time to respond.

'Applications in by the end of next week,' she says cheerily.

She didn't even ask me if I'd accepted the Conservatoire offer. She just completely assumes that I have. Now she expects me to spend time over the summer with other *exceptional* students. Strangers. My hands are actually shaking as I stuff the form into my bag.

I slip out of a side door and head home. So what if it isn't actually the end of the school day? If I'm such a wonderful model pupil, maybe I can do whatever I want.

Unfortunately, by coming out this way I have to pass the primary school, which finishes before us. There are a group of parents hanging round at the gate.

'Hi Gemma! You finished early today?' It's Rosie's mum.

'Hello Mrs Thomson.'

'It's nice to catch you alone. Rosie's really enjoying the piano lessons.'

'That's good.'

'I was wondering if you'd consider making it two lessons a week?'

I shake my head. Teaching piano hasn't been as bad as I feared, but I don't want to overdo it. 'I'm not really sure I've got time. Exams and, uh …'

'No problem, I just thought I'd ask. Are you still okay for us to come next Monday?'

I nod, smile and move on.

At the corner I turn to see the kids pouring out in all directions, running and laughing, so happy to be free. I notice that all the parents who've come to meet their offspring have kids way younger than Rosie. I wonder why her mum needed to come and meet her. They haven't lived around here long, but her route home isn't exactly difficult.

And then I remember that they live close to me, so they'll be walking in the same direction. If I don't want to have to walk with them, and make small talk, I need to hurry.

I hurry.

I let myself think over the Conservatoire offer for one more day, but I don't feel any different. It's not for me. I open up the forms on the computer, squinting so I can see the Decline button but not read anything else. I click it. A question comes up, asking me if I'm sure. Yes. I think … I click before I can change my mind and slam the laptop closed. There. It's done.

I go downstairs to make some hot chocolate. I take it into the sitting room where Mum is watching a drama on television and my older brother Liam is playing a game on his phone.

'I've just turned down the place at the Conservatoire.'

'Thought you already had,' says Liam, barely glancing up.

Mum drags her eyes away from the dead body on the screen. 'I'm glad you've decided, dear. It's a great compliment to be offered a place, but your Dad and I didn't want you to do it if it made you unhappy.'

'Thanks,' I say. But I think of all the piano and singing lessons they've paid for, all the trips to Carlisle for the orchestra, and I feel bad for not to making the most of their investment.

'You can still carry on with your music as a hobby,' says Mum. If anything, her understanding makes me feel worse.

'It was never going to be a reliable career, was it?' says Liam. He's on a training scheme with one of the banks. Doesn't sound like fun to me but he earns enough to fund his car, his computer games and his nights out, which seems to be all he cares about.

I take the rest of my drink upstairs, wondering what *I* care about and what I should do with my future. Then I get mad because I'm *seventeen*. Why do I even need to be thinking about a career right now?

Jamie

Innis and Kris have rounded me up to play five-a-side football. They're one short for this evening's session and they say if I do so much refereeing, I must know something about playing. It's nice to be asked, even if I don't even want to think about refereeing just now. Still no word from the Association. The longer this goes on, the surer I am that the outcome won't be good.

It's fun to be playing the game instead of enforcing its rules for once. The referee training means I'm fit enough to keep up with most of the others, and if my ball skills aren't brilliant then I'm not the only one. At this level, we're playing for fun and a chance to hit the bar afterwards. For once I don't overindulge, either. I'm the one leading Innis home as he meanders across the pavement.

'Don't you fucking love it when your team wins?' he asks. 'We wo-o-on!' I nudge him away from the curb and he wavers towards the building on the other side of the pavement.

'Aye,' I say. I don't have a clue if he's talking about the five-a-side team or his heroes, Barcelona. He probably doesn't either.

'You gonna join us permanently? You're a better player than the wanker who let us down.'

That's a compliment. I think. 'I can fill in if I'm free, but if I'm offered a match to ref then I have to take that.'

'Aye. Knew you were just a bloody ref at heart. Could see you agreed with that … that …' He comes to a standstill and loses his train of thought.

'Come on mate, not far now.' I nudge him forwards again. But at the same time I'm thinking, why am I even bothering? He didn't look out for me when I got wasted. And they only asked me to join the team today because they needed an extra man. He and Kris aren't real friends.

I pause and because I'm now a step in front, Innis barges into me and nearly falls over. 'Woah mate! What you standing there for?'

I lead him back to halls without saying another word. He doesn't seem to notice.

Do I actually have any real friends? I've met lots of acquaintances since I came to Glasgow, and I go out for drinks with guys from school when I'm back in Dumfries. But if I never saw any of them again, would I care? More depressingly, would they even notice?

I think of Gemma and Lily and how they've been friends for forever. How you know they'll stick up for each other whenever, wherever. I know they're girls, so it's different, but there were guys in my year at school who were good friends too. Rob Bradshaw and Kieran Smith still hang out. If I messaged either of them, I'm sure they'd be happy to meet up for a drink. But if I didn't message, they wouldn't just think to invite me.

It strikes me that for all my popularity in school, I'm no one's first choice.

Why does it matter? Why am I even thinking these stupid thoughts?

I deliver Innis to his room and he slaps me on the back. 'Hey, mate, we here already?' He stumbles inside and slams the door in my face. Not that I wanted to spend any longer in meaningless drunken conversation, but he could have offered.

Gemma

Lily says, 'So what did you decide about your Conservatoire offer?'

I hesitate before I say the words out loud. 'I declined.'

Lily looks aghast. 'No! Gemma, really?'

'Yes, really.'

'But you've got so much potential.'

'It's not what I want to do.'

'Have you told Mrs Guthrie?'

'She hasn't asked.'

'Don't you think–'

'Lily, just leave it. Okay?' Usually I'm fine with how persistent Lily can be, but right now I'm totally out of coping strategies. It not like I don't have any doubts about whether I did the right thing. I just want to make the decision, stick to it and move on.

'I'm only trying to help,' Lily insists for the thousandth time and, honestly, it's 999 times too many.

'Well you're not helping!' I shout. Thank goodness I didn't tell her about the Musicians Centre possibility – which I've now missed the deadline for.

I get up and walk out of the common room. Part of me is mortified because I know everyone is looking at us. But the other part is angry. I don't need Lily making this any more difficult.

Lily doesn't give up. She follows me out. 'I'm sorry,' she says. She's apologising? My heart lightens and then drops immediately as she adds, 'I shouldn't have brought it up in front of everyone back there. Let's find somewhere quiet where we can go and talk this over.'

'There isn't anything to talk over.'

'But it's your big chance. Do you know how many people are desperate to get into the Conservatoire?'

'Including you?' I shouldn't have said it. Lily's eyes flash with hurt. I take a deep breath. 'Look, Lily, I'm sorry you didn't get in to do Drama, but–'

'This isn't about me.'

That sets me off again. 'Well maybe it should be!'

'At least I know what I want to do instead!' Lily's shouting now too. 'You've only applied to music courses and you've just turned down the best one!'

I hate confrontation, I really do. But this time I am not backing down, 'Then maybe I just won't study music at all!'

'But don't you think–'

'Yes, Lily, I *do* think. All I do is think! The question is, do you listen?' She looks stunned. 'I've told you how

I feel but you're still going on and on about this being a great chance and how I should take it. But you know what? It doesn't matter if it's an amazing opportunity if it's not right for me! And the fact that you can't see that it's not right for me makes me wonder if you know me at all.'

Lily's mouth is hanging slightly open. I won't say we've never argued before, but I've never stood up for myself quite like this. I *am* in the right, aren't I? I'm pretty sure I am. I think I'm going to cry. She still doesn't respond.

'Forget it.' I turn and walk away.

Part of me expects Lily to call me back. I speed up just in case, but she doesn't call. Somehow that feels worse.

If I go home now I'll miss French, but I need to get away. I head out of the back gates, where a teacher is less likely to see me. I message Milly who I sit next to in French.

Gemma: Not feeling great so heading home. Can you tell Mrs McColl?

Milly: No problem. I think we're just carrying on with that weird Eluard poem.

For a moment, I almost regret ducking out. I liked that poem. I'm not sure I understand it, but some of the words resonate with me. It's about being a creature behind a curtain, that one no one sees or hears. Sometimes I think that's me.

Jamie

In early February I get the bus down to Dumfries so I can spend the weekend at home. Mum's been going on at me to visit, and as I'm still not reffing I don't have that excuse. In a way I'm quite looking forward to the break. Glasgow has definitely lost its gloss. No football, too much studying, and now I'm putting the hours in, there's no doubt about it – this course really isn't for me.

Maybe I'll get to see some of my school friends, if any of them are home. Or Gemma. But meeting her for coffee or something, which seemed obvious and straightforward in Glasgow, doesn't seem so easy in Newton St Cuthbert. There are only a couple of coffee shops and we'd be bound to be seen. That doesn't bother me, exactly, it just makes things feel different.

The Friday afternoon bus is packed and by the time it gets to the Whitesands in Dumfries, I'm hot and sweaty and not in the greatest mood. Fortunately, Dad's the one who's come to pick me up. He doesn't attack me with a barrage of questions. Just 'Journey all right?'

'Not bad.'

Then we get into the car and drive off in silence.

We're almost in Newton St Cuthbert before we speak again. Dad says, 'Good you could come home for a visit. Your mother misses you boys.'

'Michael's coming too, isn't he?'

'No, he said he might, but then his plans changed.'

There's not the slightest hint of criticism in what he says, but I know Mum has built up to this visit and had all sorts of ideas for having the four of us together for the first time since Christmas. For once, it looks like I'm going to be the son that's doing the right thing.

The satisfaction this thought brings doesn't last long. By Saturday afternoon I've had more than enough of Mum and her helpful suggestions. Morag Leslie and some of her crowd are home, so I go out for drinks with them on Saturday evening. That means I'm pretty hungover on Sunday morning and not at all keen on going out for the special family breakfast Mum has planned.

'It's a new place that's opened up near Sandhead,' she says happily. 'They do all sorts of outdoor activities and their café is top-notch. I've been trying to get your dad out there for ages, but he's always so busy.'

I open my eyes briefly and meet Dad's in the rear-view mirror. I bet he's wishing he was on call right now. This place will be noisy and probably full of his patients. That's definitely one of the downsides of living in a small town. I don't know how Dad puts up with it, actually. Everyone knows him, everyone's always kind of watching him. I think Mum loves it, being the wife of the senior partner in the GP practice. If she could get away with it, she'd probably wave to people as she passed in the car.

I don't know why I'm thinking all these things about her now. I used to just accept that was the way she was. Now I want to shout at her to shut up.

The café is okay, kind of posh rustic, and the food looks delicious. I order the Full Scottish Breakfast but then my stupid stomach rebels on me and I push the plate away half-full.

'Jamie, you haven't finished,' Mum says. 'You shouldn't order what you can't eat.'

I thought I'd wolf it down. Good cure for a hangover and all that. Maybe those shots at the end of last night weren't such a good idea.

'If you're not going to eat your tattie scone,' says Dad, homing in on it before Mum can stop him. She'd made him choose from the healthy menu.

She frowns and then turns back to me. 'You've scarcely eaten anything. It's such a waste.'

'Yeah, yeah, think of all the starving children in Africa.'

'Jamie! There's no need to be rude.'

'I was just saving you the trouble of finishing your spiel. I've heard it often enough. It's not like what I eat here is going to make any difference there, is it? And why the starving children in Africa? Why not starving children in Scotland? They do exist, you know.'

Mum glares. 'I don't know what's got into you. You've been like a bear with a sore head all weekend.'

So that's what I get for trying to make an effort. 'You wanted me to come home, didn't you? Maybe I shouldn't have bothered, like Michael didn't.'

'Of course we wanted you to come home. And Michael would have come if he could have. At least when he is home he has proper conversations with us.'

'Good for him. At least you've got one perfect son.'

'Don't be silly, Jamie. All I'm saying is that whenever you visit these days you're either in your bedroom or out with your friends. Why can't you spend more time with us?'

'Because every time I spend more than two minutes with you, I'm subjected to twenty questions!' Besides, I'm not out with friends all the time. How can I be when they've all moved away?

Mum is pretending to be hurt now. 'I'm sorry you think we ask too many questions. But if you told us more about your life, we wouldn't need to.'

I don't give myself time to think better of it. 'You want to know what's been going on in my life, do you?' I say, roughly.

'You don't need to raise your voice,' says Mum, glancing about to see who might be listening.

I'm past caring. 'I'll tell you what's been going on. I've been drinking too much and not studying enough, and I'm so far behind with my assignments I'm probably about to be kicked off the course. And that's on top of having failed *two* subjects in the first semester. I didn't go to my Grade Eight exam because what's the point? Who cares about Duke of Edinburgh these days? And the first non-youth match I reffed was such a disaster, I'll probably be put back down to kids if I'm not let go all together.'

I pause for breath. Both my parents are staring at me. Dad is frowning slightly. Mum gets in first with, 'They can't ask you to leave your course. You did really well to get in. You had lots of other offers.'

'They can if I haven't been attending lectures or submitting assignments. Read the small print, Mum.'

'Why didn't you tell us before? There must be something we can do. You have a study supervisor, don't you? I'll phone him first thing–'

'That's why I didn't tell you! Because you always want to take over.'

'I'm only trying to help ...'

As Mum trails off Dad has the chance to say, 'And why are you behind with your assignments?'

Sometimes I forget that Dad is the really switched on one. That's probably what makes him such a good GP, the ability to spot the important things.

I don't meet his gaze. 'I just can't seem to concentrate on them. I'm not really enjoying the course.'

'You don't have to enjoy the course,' says Mum. 'It's a means to an end. Do you think Michael is enjoying all those lectures on anatomy and what have you?'

'We're not talking about Michael, we're talking about me.'

Mum looks around again and says, 'Perhaps we can talk about this a bit more when we get home. Maybe if you did less refereeing–'

'I told you, I'm not refereeing anymore! And there's nothing to talk about. I've decided.' And suddenly, apparently, I have. I'm done struggling to be a good student on a 'sensible' course. Even when I make an effort – and I really have been this term – I just can't do it. Gemma's right. There's no point in doing what everyone expects of you if it's not what *you* want. 'I'm dropping out. I don't want to study this crap. I don't want to be an accountant or work in business.'

'You can't just drop out ...'

'Watch me.' I wipe my mouth with a paper serviette and toss it aside. I feel relieved. Euphoric almost. No more Glasgow. No more studying. I'm going to be free.

Gemma

After twelve years of friendship, going back to practically our first day at primary school, Lily and I aren't talking. Or rather, we talk if we have to, but we don't really say anything. I wasn't the one who started all this, so Lily should definitely be the one to apologise. But so far she's shown absolutely no sign of that.

At lunchtime on Monday I get a call from Mrs Thomson. I presume she's phoning to cancel the lesson, which would be a shame. Doing that straight after school means I wouldn't have time to miss hanging out with Lily instead. Plus I'm quite enjoying teaching Rosie. She's mastered the basic exercises and I was planning to move her on to some easy tunes next.

'Gemma, I wonder if you could do me a favour?'

'Er,' I say. That question has got me into quite a few annoying situations – like teaching piano in the first place.

'I thought about it when I saw you walking past the primary school the other day. My mum or I try to be there to meet Rosie but I'm going to be pushed for time today. Is there any chance you could meet her yourself, and then walk with her back to your house for the lesson?'

'I suppose,' I say, wondering why on earth that should be necessary.

'That's so kind of you. I really appreciate it.' Before she rings off she makes sure I know what time primary school ends, and gets me to promise I'll be waiting at the gate before the bell goes.

I'm waiting at the gate as instructed when Rosie appears. She's not walking with any of the other kids and even though her head is down, she's so tall she towers above them.

'Hiya,' I say, when she's within hearing distance.

She glances up, gives a small sigh of relief and falls into step beside me. The other kids are rushing around us, shouting, crossing the road without looking and generally being a nuisance.

'How's school?' I ask awkwardly.

'Okay.'

'When did you start here?'

'In August.'

We walk along in silence for a while. She's clearly very shy. I remember clearly how I felt at her age. I *never* spoke to strangers. I've got nothing against silence, but I'm older and therefore feel like I should try and make her feel at ease.

'I've been thinking about what music we should move you on to. What kind of music do you like listening to? Now you've done those practice pieces, you can choose something different if you want.'

A long pause. 'Not sure.'

Jeez, I don't remember her being this difficult during lessons. Or maybe I just didn't notice because all she had to do was what I asked her to.

I wrack my brains for current pop groups but come up with a big fat blank. I'm more into folk and classical music. Even the more modern stuff I listen to, like Emily Smith or Jellyman's Daughter, aren't exactly chart material.

'Think about it, anyway,' I say, then let the conversation lapse until we get to my house. If she's not bothered by it, I suppose there's no reason I should be.

Toby helps break the ice once we get to my house. Rosie had been nervous of him at first, but now she wants to pat him before every lesson. Toby leans against her, enjoying the attention.

In the absence of Rosie's own music suggestions, I decide on something neutral.

'Why don't we try learning 'Hot Cross Buns'?' I say brightly. 'I want you to try singing as well as playing. It helps if you sing the song as well.'

She looks at me with wide, dark eyes.

'Actually, I've no idea if that's true but Mrs Marshall always said it, so it might be.'

I get a small smile in response. Better than nothing.

'Okay, go over the practice pieces I set you, and then we'll start the singing.'

Weirdly, the singing seems to relax her. She sings with me first, then without, to see if she can carry the simple melody. She's got a cute voice, soft but it holds a note well.

'Brilliant. Right, now you're going to play some of the notes, too. Careful of your fingering. We'll start slowly ...'

The more Rosie relaxes, the more she seems willing to speak, even if it's only to ask or answer a question. It's hard to tell, but I think her mum is right and she does enjoy these lessons.

Her mum's a bit late to pick her up, so when I think she's done enough for the day I take Rosie into the kitchen so she can make a fuss of Toby some more.

I say cautiously, 'Were you okay earlier, when I picked you up from school?'

She's a nice kid. I don't like to think of her being miserable.

'Yeah.'

We're back to minimal answers. Fortunately her mum arrives a few minutes later.

Jamie

My euphoria at quitting uni doesn't last. By Monday morning it's dissipated under the relentless pressure of Mum's disappointment, which so far is mostly silent but I'm sure that won't last either. And really, I didn't think this through. Even if I am sure I don't want to continue with Accounting and Business Studies, I have absolutely no idea what I do want to do.

I'm determined to quit the course, though. I can't stick another lecture, let alone another failed assignment. I head back to Glasgow on Tuesday to see the course administrator and tell her I'm quitting. She tries to persuade me to think things over, to go and see Graham, to chat things through. As though any of that would make a difference. I tell her I've discussed this with my parents and the decision is made. I don't tell her they're furious and also hoping I'll change my mind.

Then I go back to halls and start packing up my stuff. I don't need to move it all out at once. The hall fees are paid until the end of May, which is another thing Mum is annoyed about. The government pays the tuition, but Mum and Dad have been paying for my accommodation. Now it's all going to be wasted. I do feel bad about that.

At least I don't see anything of Innis and the others. They're all at lectures, or still asleep. I wonder how long it'll take them to notice I've gone.

I get most of my stuff into three bags and haul them out to the car, which Mum has reluctantly lent me for the day. That just leaves my guitar in its case on top of the wardrobe. Definitely don't want to leave that. I sling it over my shoulder and head off.

When I get home I make the opposite journey, lugging all the stuff up to my childhood bedroom, the place I thought I'd escaped only six months ago.

I collapse on my bed, not even bothering to unpack, and try to summon the enthusiasm for any of the things I'd thought about doing with this amazing free time: travelling, getting a job, playing more guitar, listening to more music, partying. I can't. I feel like a complete failure.

Mum shouts up that she's made a pot of tea and why don't I come down? I shout okay, because if I don't she'll probably come and haul me out. There are going to be days and days of this. Just Mum and me in the house. So much for freedom.

As I go downstairs, Lucy, our mad Labrador, comes dashing up, obviously hoping I'm going to take her for a walk. That feels doable. Actually, Lucy might be getting quite a lot of walks in the near future.

Gemma

Tuesday, Lily is extra busy and extra chatty with everyone but me. It's like she's the one who's offended. I notice Tom looking from her to me a couple of times, but I'm not sure anyone else has noticed. I'm always sort of in the background. Now I'm even more so.

There's no one home when I get in from school, except Toby who heaves himself to his feet, exhales a massive sigh, and staggers over to greet me. No matter how hard it is for him, Toby will always make the effort. I drop down to the floor and fling my arms around his smelly neck. His coat is still thick, but underneath I can feel he's lost even more weight. I rock him to and fro. 'We've got to feed you up, Toby boy. We've got to keep you strong.'

He gives another sigh, so I get the full effect of his doggy breath, and takes himself back to his basket.

I go and wash my hands. I adore Toby, but he's not exactly hygienic.

By five o'clock there's still no one else home, so it looks like I'm going to have to feed Toby and take him for his evening walk. It's more of a shuffle than a walk, but it has to be done. And getting out of the house will be nicer than sitting and worrying about Lily.

I pick up Toby's lead and he does an excited hop, because he still thinks going for a walk is fun. He almost falls over, but manages to save himself and totters over for me to attach the lead to his collar. I don't know why I even bother with a lead. He's not likely to run off these days, but I'd never forgive myself if something happened to him.

I decide to take him into the woods at the back of the houses. It's a bit far for him (meaning more than five minutes) but at this time of year it'll be quiet, and quiet is what I want.

I'm not much into exercise, but Toby's pace is slow even for me. We've reached the woods and now he wants to sniff at every bush and tree trunk. 'Come on!' I tug at his lead, but not too hard.

I hear footsteps behind and jump at the surprise of someone else being there. A voice says, 'I don't think that dog actually wants to walk.'

I swing round, and find myself face to face with Jamie. I blurt out, 'What are you doing here?' I can't believe I've bumped into him like this. I hope I'm not blushing.

He looks momentarily uncomfortable, but then he spreads his hands wide and points to the Labrador he has with him. 'Walking the dog?'

'Yes, but …' I want to ask why he's at home, why he's not at uni. But I'm fed up of people asking me difficult questions and his faint discomfort signals that maybe he won't be keen on me doing the same.

'What's her name?' I ask instead. She's a beautiful young yellow lab. I remember when his family got her. I'd seen all the puppy pictures via Lily.

'Lucy. She's not bad, is she?' He grins and bends down to unclip the lead. 'Mum says she's good at recall now. I suppose there's only one way to find out.'

The dog starts sniffing around, tail madly wagging. She tries to greet Toby but gets a half-hearted snarl for her troubles and runs on unabashed. Jamie stays beside me, like he's waiting for me to walk on, so we can go together. This is only the second time I've ever been alone with him. My heart flutters nervously.

I unclip Toby's lead. That way I'll be able to move faster than a snail's pace. 'I don't think this one's in any danger of running off.' I move on and Jamie falls into step beside me. We have to keep stopping to allow Toby to catch up, but Jamie doesn't seem to mind.

I steal a glance at him every now and then to check that he really is here. Meeting up in Glasgow seemed different, not quite real. But here, dressed in torn jeans and a hoodie, his light brown hair curling into his collar, his fringe growing out and falling into his eyes, he seems all too real. He looks good. Less neat and tidy than he used to, but still as ridiculously handsome. Meanwhile I'm in school uniform with my horrible grey duffle coat over the top. It's warm and practical but I wish I'd chosen something more stylish.

We stop beside a large, marshy pond and Lucy comes rushing back, all excited. Jamie sighs and says, 'Okay.' He picks up some stones and starts hurling them one at a time out into the water. The dog is beside herself with delight, rushing in, rushing back out and then in again.

Toby stands at the water's edge, looking bemused. I can remember a time when he would have been swimming about like Lucy, loving it. Poor Toby. I pick up a small branch and show it to him and then toss it about twenty centimetres. His whole shaggy body quivers with excitement and he throws himself forwards into the shallows. He just manages to reach the branch and then collapses with the shock of it all.

Jamie bursts out laughing. 'Call that a dog?'

I can't help laughing too, even as I protest, 'I bet yours won't be so lively when she's thirteen.' I encourage Toby to get to his feet, which he does laboriously, and then toss a stick just ahead of his nose, a tiny bit further in. I'm definitely not going to rescue him if he goes too deep.

We stay by the pond for a while. The dogs are happy and it's funny watching them, one so lively, the other barely moving. Eventually Toby staggers back out and tries to shake himself. He topples over from the effort. Oh dear. I hope he'll manage the walk home.

'Is he all right?' asks Jamie.

'Not sure.' I pat the dog's wet head and he looks at me adoringly. He doesn't seem the least bit upset that he's flat on his tummy. I help him up, which is messy. 'I think I better head back. Slowly.'

'We'll come with you.' Jamie whistles. The lab comes haring towards us, spraying us both with water.

'Yuck!' I say, jumping back when it's already too late.

'Looks like she has learnt recall,' says Jamie, grinning.

We follow the path back down the hill. Just before we reach my estate, Jamie branches off. His family live in one of the big detached houses further out of town.

He raises a hand. 'See you.' And then he's gone.

Jamie

Being back at home is even more horrendous than I feared. Dad is wearing his most patient expression and making a thing of not pressuring me. Mum, on the other hand, can't stop making suggestions. And, at some point I'm going to have to face the fact that everyone will want to know why I'm back, and if I tell them they'll know what a failure I am.

'You'll need to get a job, you know,' says Mum. 'You can't expect us to support you if you're not studying. Do you want me to have a word with Dad's practice manager, see if they've got any vacancies?'

Can't she see this is why it all went wrong in the first place: because she wants to make all the decisions?

I only get as far as, 'Er–' before she continues.

'And if you want to do a different course at university next year, you need to start thinking about it straight away. Otherwise you'll miss the deadline. One of my friends is a career adviser, do you want me to make an appointment with her?'

'Not right now,' I say quickly. She frowns, but puts her phone back in her pocket. Jesus.

I need to find out what it is I *am* interested in before I choose another course. And currently I have no idea what that is. It's hard to think about anything when Mum just keeps talking at me.

'… And, Jamie, the least you can do is help around the house. You did your own washing while you were away, so there's no reason why you shouldn't do it here …'

As predicted, I end up taking Lucy for *a lot* of walks just to get out of the house, but after that first day I don't see Gemma again. That's a shame. I feel like she's someone I could maybe bounce some ideas off of.

I can't spend all my time at home or in the woods, so I'm bound to meet other people eventually. Lily is probably the person I want to see least, so obviously I bump right into her when I go down to the Post Office to post a parcel for Mum.

'Hey, hello. How are you? What you doing at home mid-week?'

'It's Friday.'

'So it is. School life's such fun I must've lost track of the days.' She mock yawns so I know she's joking.

'Speaking of school,' I say, dodging her question, 'why aren't you there?' It's mid-morning, which was one of the reasons I'd agreed to come and do Mum's chores.

'Free period,' says Lily. 'That's one of the advantages of Sixth Form, if you cast your mind back.'

'As I remember, unless it's first or last period, you're supposed to stay in school.'

She waves her hand to dismiss that. I know none of us really stuck to it either, but her confidence still irritates me. I might have *looked* confident before, but I was never as effortlessly sure of myself as Lily.

The queue moves forwards and it's my turn at the counter. Unfortunately, when I finish Lily's waiting for me. She walks with me out of the shop. 'How's uni going? I haven't seen you since the Student Union.' She grins. Trust her to bring that up.

Since she's asked point blank, I might as well tell her the truth. Then she'll tell the whole town and I won't need to discuss it again.

I keep my tone calm. 'I decided Accounting and Business Studies wasn't the course for me.'

'So you've dropped out?'

Calm. Measured. 'I've decided not to continue, yes.'

'Wow.' She stops and turns to look at me, and by the sheer force of her personality I find myself stopping too. 'Well that is a surprise. What did your mum say?'

I shrug. I'm sure she can imagine just what Mum said.

In the distance we hear the school bell ring. 'Shit. I better go.' She's already walking backwards away from me as she talks. 'See you around, maybe?' Then she turns and runs.

That could have gone worse. At least you can rely on Lily not to spare you much sympathy – which is the last thing I need. Plus it occurs to me that Gemma doesn't appear to have mentioned seeing me earlier in the week. I thought she and Lily told each other everything. I wonder what it means that I'm the exception.

Gemma

It's been more than a week since Lily and I fell out. For once I don't do anything to mend fences. I'm still annoyed with her for being so sure she knows what's best for me. It's my life, isn't it? Even if I don't know what I want to do with it.

On Friday lunchtime Lily wanders into the Sixth Form common room and says, 'Did you know Jamie dropped out of uni?'

She's talking to a whole group of us, which includes Rory Mackenzie, this year's head boy, and some of his friends, so I don't need to answer. I'm definitely listening, though.

Donny says, 'Wowee. Really?'

'Apparently. Who would have thought it?'

I can't help saying, 'Are you sure?' It seems so unlikely. Jamie, who's always great at everything he tries, *quitting*?

'That's what he said. I met him at the Post Office

this morning and asked why he wasn't at uni.'

I'm a bit hurt. I'd also asked Jamie why he wasn't at uni when I saw him earlier in the week, but he didn't answer me.

Rory says, 'Why would he drop out?'

Lily shrugs. 'I don't know. For attention?'

Tom says, 'It's not that unusual. Sometimes people from small towns struggle in a big city. Or decide they've chosen the wrong course.'

That's one of the many things I like about Tom. He's just so sensible. When he puts it like that, it doesn't sound so bad. I'm annoyed with Lily for being so flippant. Not everyone finds things as easy as she does.

I say, 'It's a shame for him, that it hasn't worked out.'

'Sometimes it's good for people to know what failure feels like,' says Tom, which makes me remember that for all his sensible points, he never liked Jamie much. And that was before he and Lily started going out.

Someone shouts to Tom and the others drift away. Now it's just Lily, me and an awkward silence. One I refuse to fill in case offering the first olive branch means admitting some kind of blame.

Just as it seems like the silence will continue indefinitely, Rory comes back. 'Aren't we supposed to be seeing Mr Barrett?' he says to Lily, who promptly goes off with him. It'll be some head girl/head boy thing, but it feels like she's happy to have the excuse to leave.

I spend most of the weekend in Carlisle. It's my last ever performance with the Junior Orchestra. I think I might miss that, playing when you're part of something bigger and the attention isn't only on you. After this year I'll be too old for it. I hate getting older.

Mum and I stay with Gran while we're there, which means we get completely spoilt. So all in all, it's not a bad weekend. There's no time to miss Lily at all.

On Monday I've got Rosie for another piano lesson. As usual she doesn't say much, but she works diligently and by the end of the lesson we've moved on from singing 'Hot Cross Buns' to 'Coulter's Candy'. She still hasn't suggested any music she likes, so we're sticking with the traditional songs I learnt when I started. It's a nice change from the complicated stuff I'm doing for Advanced Higher Music.

'How's school?' I say when the lesson has finished and we're waiting for her mum to arrive. She lives so close that I don't know why Rosie can't just walk home on her own.

''S okay.'

'I've always wanted to go in and look around since they fixed it up. It looks so much nicer than when I went.'

She doesn't respond.

'It's got so many more windows now, and everything is so brightly painted. Is the playground as fun as it looks? Not that I would have been brave enough to try those climbing frames, of course. My friend Lil–' I stop because I don't want to think about Lily and how she's acting like *I'm* the one to blame for our falling out.

Rosie mutters something.

'What was that?'

She's looking at the piano keys, not at me. 'I hate school. I *hate* it.' And she starts to cry. Not great, heaving sobs, but silent tears that stream down her face.

I'm completely at a loss. 'I suppose none of us really like school ...'

She sniffs.

'Is there – is there any reason you hate it?' I say cautiously.

She stops crying as suddenly as she started and scrubs her eyes with a tissue. Her shoulders are hunched away from me. She shrinks further when I put out a hand to comfort her.

'Can you tell me what's wrong?' I say helplessly.

She gives a tiny shake of her head. 'No.'

I'm completely out of my depth, so I give up on the questions and just take her to the bathroom so she can wash her face. At the sound of the doorbell she says fiercely, 'Don't tell Mum.'

'It's okay, I won't.' If that's the only thing I can do for her, then I'll do it.

When she's gone I sit in the music room alone, trying to work out how I could have acted differently. I hate to think of Rosie being unhappy, but if she won't tell me anything then what can I do? It's so easy for Lily to ask questions and get involved, but it's not for me.

I need to stop thinking about Lily. Now that I'm at a loose end, I can't help wondering what she's doing. As far as I've seen (not that I've been checking) she hasn't come over to Tom's recently. I could probably go and hang out with Sarah, or (more sensibly) get on with my French essay, but I don't.

Instead I do what I've been wanting to do all weekend. I message Jamie.

Gemma: Lily says you've given up uni. Hope everything is OK.

I feel so bad for him. I get the impression his mum is quite pushy and expects a lot. She's certainly all over him when he does well, like all his head boy stuff last year and when he won the talent show in the summer. I'm grateful all over again for how laid back my parents are.

My phone vibrates.

Jamie: I'm fine. How are you?

Gemma: Fine. Bored. Trying to think of some excuse not to do my French homework.

As soon as I send the message, I worry that he'll think I'm angling to spend time with him. (OK, maybe I *am* angling to spend time with him, I just don't want it to be *obvious*.)

Gemma: Mum wants me to go over to see my aunt with her so I might do that.

(That visit is tomorrow but he doesn't need to know the details.)

Jamie: I thought I'd take Lucy for a walk along the river. You could come if you want?

I can feel my cheeks flush. Of course I want!

Jamie

Is it weird that Gemma Anderson is the one person who seems interested in spending time with me? Maybe she feels sorry for me. Since I spoke to Lily in the Post Office, I feel like I've got this big sign over me saying *LOOK! FAILURE!* but no one has actually got in touch. Either they don't care or they don't want to be tarred with the same brush.

I've only ever known Gemma as that quiet friend of Lily's. Now I know she's thoughtful and funny and, okay, she seems to quite like me. She seems happy to spend time with me, and that makes me really want to spend time with her.

We take the path that leads along the riverbank, away from the sea. We don't say much. At first there are a few other people around, mostly dog walkers, but after a while it's just us. It's a cold day, with the water running dark and slow, and the sky grey and brooding. The path starts to get a bit muddy and Lucy capers about through the puddles. Occasionally she veers towards the water and looks at me hopefully, but when I say no she backs off, tail still wagging.

Gemma says, 'I like that dogs are so happy. Even if it's cold and they're not allowed to do the one thing they really want, they're still happy.'

'Lucy doesn't really want to go in that river. She just thinks she does.'

Gemma gives a small shudder. She's walking on the side of the path farthest from the water, like she's frightened of it. 'She might get swept away, mightn't she?'

'She'd probably be okay. But if she wasn't, I definitely don't fancy going in to rescue her.'

We carry on in silence for a while, Lucy running back every so often, her tongue lolling out like she's grinning.

I say, 'It'll be nice when spring eventually comes.'

'I know. A bit of warmth. Longer days.'

'And the sailing club will start again. I didn't get the chance to go out much last summer. I missed it. Do you sail?'

'No. Not my kind of thing.'

'You should try. It's fun.'

'That's what Lily says.' Gemma sighs. 'She got really into it last year, arranging the regatta and everything.'

'I could teach you to sail, if you want,' I say. 'Once the weather improves.'

'No. I mean, thanks, but no.' She shudders again.

'It's great. There's a kind of freedom to being out on the water.'

'I don't like water.' She says it quietly but very firmly. I glance across at her and she's biting her lip and looking worried. She seems to be shivering. 'You cold? D'you want to turn back?'

'No, I'm fine.' She gestures to her coat, a bulky grey duffle. 'This might not be fashionable but it's definitely warm.' She pulls her bobble hat low over her ears, as though to emphasise how warm her clothing is. She looks really cute, all bundled up so you can hardly see the red hair, her cheeks pink with the cold.

By the time we part to go our separate ways I'm feeling almost cheerful. But the closer I get to my house the slower my feet become, and I end up taking Lucy on an extra loop around the block. I'm dreading the aimless weeks ahead, stuck under Mum's magnifying glass. If I leave off getting home until Dad finishes golf, I might at least survive today.

Gemma

I've finally told Mrs Guthrie that I won't be going to the Conservatoire. I had to when she said to me, 'I want to do a special assembly on careers in music. I'd like you to be part of it.'

She was stunned. 'Are you sure, Gemma? This is a big opportunity you're turning down. Have you discussed it with Mrs Marshall?' And on and on until I just wanted to run away and cry. I said I was sorry lots of times. But I wasn't sorry enough to let her make me change my mind.

A week later, I get a call from Mrs Thomson asking if I can give Rosie's lesson at her own house rather than mine. I'm not sure why the sudden change but I message back to say yes, and to check their house number. When I get there Mrs Thomson shows me in, looking even more pinched and worried than usual.

'Can I just have a quick word?' she says, and ushers me into the kitchen before I can answer. She closes the door. 'Just to warn you, I don't know what's wrong with Rosie. She refused to go to school today. In fact, she refused to even get dressed. I said I'd cancel your lesson, too, but she got so upset I said I'd ask you to come here. I'm so grateful you agreed.'

'It's fine,' I say. 'Is Rosie not well?'

'She won't say.'

'Maybe she's finding it hard to settle in at her new school ...' I think of Rosie saying "I hate school" so desperately. Should I have told her mum?

'She wasn't happy at her old school either. I don't know what– She's coming downstairs.' Mrs Thomson pushes the door back open and tries to pretend I've just that second arrived, which I clearly haven't unless I came in through the garden. Rosie doesn't say anything, though. She just hunches her dressing gown around her and leads me to where their piano is kept.

As I follow her, I wonder if she really is ill. Maybe she's like Sarah, where you don't look ill but everything is secretly such hard work.

After about half an hour of the lesson, I ask, 'Are you feeling okay?'

She shrugs. Her face is mostly hidden behind her hair.

'Hey, if you're not feeling up to it, we don't need to do any more today.'

She doesn't respond.

'You're doing so well, you know.' I've read somewhere that positive reinforcement is important.

Lily was always really positive about the things I did, from my music to silly things like baking the best cupcakes EVER (according to her). It might have been annoying at times, but maybe now I can understand her reasons. I wonder if I was ever as difficult to talk to as Rosie is?

Rosie mumbles something. She's as bad as I am at not speaking up.

'Sorry?'

'I'm not going back.'

'Oh.' I'm immediately out of my depth. 'Aye, school can be a bit of a pain. I think it's friends that make it kind of bearable.' I pause, feeling a sudden pang for Lily.

'I don't have any friends.'

I pat her cautiously on the shoulder and she shrinks away like she did at my house. It's awful. Rosie is so unhappy, and I don't know how to help.

I say, 'Of course you have friends. You have me, don't you?'

She glances at me. 'No one likes me.'

'Of course they like you. You're lovely.'

She doesn't respond to that at all, just grasps her hands together so tightly her knuckles are white.

If her mum's listening she'll have noticed the lack of any piano playing. I don't want her to come in and find Rosie like this. I play a couple of scales slowly, and then I show Rosie how to do them. 'Come on, you need to practise getting your little finger to do more work.'

I'm such a coward, but I don't know what else to do. We get to the end of the lesson without any more discussion. As we finish I say, 'You know, if you wanted to fit in an extra lesson this week, I could come round again on Thursday or Friday.'

'Maybe,' she whispers. 'Thanks.'

I walk home tense and gloomy. How can someone so young be so alone? Rosie makes me realise how lucky I was to have Lily in my life when I was as young and as shy as her. Tom and Sarah too, of course, but Lily was the force of nature that meant it was impossible to be left out.

As I think that, Tom appears round the corner ahead of me. I'm pleased. We can walk home together. I haven't seen much of him lately because of the way things are with Lily. Now we can chat about school and complain about homework and I don't need to worry about Rosie. Or Lily.

When we reach our houses, I expect him to head off inside, but he hesitates. 'Er, Gem?'

'Yeah?'

'What's wrong? You know, between you and Lily?'

Perhaps I do have to worry about Lily. And I don't want to. 'Maybe you should ask her.'

'I did. She said you need a bit of time to think things over, but everything's *fine*.' He puts up his hands to make speech quotes when he says "fine", like he doesn't believe it is. The first part of the sentence removes any possible sympathy I might have felt for Lily.

'I don't need time to think anything over. Jesus!' I can't believe Lily still believes *I'm* the one who needs to change. I can't talk about this now, it'll make me too upset, so I say, 'Just forget about it. I'm sure it will be fine.'

I'm not sure at all. I've been waiting for Lily to apologise, to accept that she was wrong. It looks like I might be waiting a long time.

Tom doesn't press the point. He heads inside his house and I go into mine. Once I'm in my bedroom, I take out my phone. Lily and I used to message each other all the time, but the date on our last messages is weeks ago.

Not my fault.

I wrench my thoughts back to Rosie and look up problems that might explain her behaviour. It makes for depressing reading. Thank goodness I didn't know Dr Google when I was her age. It would have given me even more to worry about.

Jamie

Mum says, 'I've spoken to the manager at your father's practice. She says she's looking for someone to do clerical work and she's happy to give you a try.'

'Jesus, Mum, did you think to check with me first?'

'I've given you weeks to find something for yourself.'

'Finding a job takes more than a couple of weeks.' Although, it would help if I'd actually started looking.

'It didn't take *me* long. It'll just be filing and general helping out, but you'll be earning a wage.'

I imagine going in to work with Dad, being the boss's son. I'm pretty sure all the other clerical staff are female, and mostly about twenty years older than me. But really the main thing that bothers me is that, once again, Mum has decided my fate.

'It'll only be a few hours a day,' Mum adds. 'You can do it while you're looking for something better. If there is anything better for someone with no qualifications.' She presses her lips together. I'm clearly such a disappointment. 'I said you'd start next Monday.'

I groan.

'And maybe you could have a haircut, or at least a shave, before you start? I know beards are all the fashion, but really ...'

I leave the room. It's all about appearance for Mum. She looks so neat and tidy every minute of every day: hair, nails, make up, clothes. Immaculate. The house is the same, even the garden. I bet she's only worried about me getting a job because of what people might say if I don't. Me dropping out of uni definitely won't have fitted in with her idea of us as the picture-perfect bloody family.

Michael was home at the weekend and even he said I need to get out of here soon or she'll drive me mad. He's right. I've got a vague idea about getting a summer job in France or Spain. But that's months away so I suppose I'll have to put up with being a skivvy at the medical practice for now.

Then I receive a message from the Referees' Association. Shit. Probably more bad news.

It's a request for me to ref games in Glasgow this coming Wednesday and Sunday. I click on the website to see what has happened with the complaint and all the information I get is "Case Closed". Just like that, I'm back on the list. Not that I was ever officially removed, just temporarily suspended. And both games are for kids. But I'm back to reffing!

But I no longer live in Glasgow. Do I really want to make the round trip from Newton St Cuthbert two times in a week? What they pay me won't even cover the cost of petrol. I message back saying that I'm away at the moment. Serves them right. I'm still put out by that bloody complaint and the fact that they didn't even try to hear my side.

I flop down on my bed, triumph evaporating. After a while I pick up my guitar and start strumming. I don't have to hold back here like I did in halls. Our house is pretty soundproof, otherwise Mum would've been poking her head in every ten minutes since I left uni, demanding to know why I was playing instead of working on my CV.

I strum a little harder, part of me wishing I'd taken up drums, so I could really put the walls to the test. I remember jamming in the school music room with Angus and Kieran; Owen bringing us home on the triangle while wearing a tambourine on his head. Those were the days.

Suddenly, I clap my palm over the strings to quiet them.

I've just had an idea.

Not the kind of idea Mum wants me to have; one where I sort myself out, find direction and "make the difficult choices". Nope.

I'm going to start a band.

I always wanted to, but I was too busy at school doing all the things everyone said I *should* do, like piano lessons and sailing. And that's when I wasn't studying hard to get good grades, in order to get into a good university, onto a good course, which would set me up for a good life. Only that last part never happened.

Whatever. I held up my end. Maybe now I finally get to do what I *want* to. I could play guitar or sing, or both. I'll need to find a drummer. I think Michael's drum kit is still out in the old garage, we could use that as a practice room like he used to. And I kind of like the idea of a band with a keyboard player, like Goldheart Assembly or Hurts. Who could–

Idea number two: Gemma. She's a brilliant singer and pianist. She could do keyboards and/or help out on vocals. She'll know all the local kids who do music. There's bound to be some aspiring drummer out there.

I'm keen to get started but she'll be at school right now. I message her to see if we can meet later. I suggest walking the dogs. Now I just need to figure out how to bring up the band idea without scaring her off.

Gemma

School's not great just now. I feel like I've let Mrs Guthrie down and things still aren't good with Lily. We've always been together until now. I miss it. Sometimes I miss it enough to wonder why I'm letting this go on. Maybe I should be the one to apologise. But when I think that, I also think *Why should I?*

And because I'm seeing less of Lily, I'm seeing less of Tom too. It's not like anyone's planning it, it just happens that way. Partly because I wouldn't feel comfortable talking about Lily with him. At least Jamie seems happy to hang out with me. That makes a difference. I've always thought of Jamie as, well, someone special. Someone to admire. Someone who would never speak to me. But now we're spending time together and I'm surprised by how well we get on.

There's something a bit odd today, though. We're walking in the woods just with Lucy. Poor old Toby is having a rest. Jamie keeps shooting me looks. It's making me nervous.

'You ever thought of being in a band?' he asks out of nowhere.

'What?'

'Sorry. I meant to introduce the idea slowly.'

'It's okay,' I say, although I'm still mystified.

Jamie shouts at Lucy who comes lolloping back into view. He says, 'You know Mark and Rob had a band while we were at school? And Chris Rawlings and some of his mates? It's something I always really wanted to do.'

'So why didn't you?'

He sighs. 'It didn't fit in with my mum's idea of what I should be doing for extracurriculars.'

It's strange to think of Jamie being bossed about by his mum. He always seemed to do just what he wanted to; he was so sure about everything. He doesn't seem so sure anymore. I think his experience at uni, and dropping out of uni, has changed him. Maybe that's why it's easier for us to spend time together.

'Anyway,' he continues, 'I thought it was something I might try now. But most people I know are away at uni, or they're not musical, and you play the piano so …'

'Piano isn't really a band kind of instrument,' I say quickly. I'm amazed he's even thought of involving me. And horrified at the idea of being up on stage, performing. That's one of the reasons why I didn't take up the place at the Conservatoire.

'But a keyboard is, which is basically the same thing. I've got a keyboard at home that you could use.'

This is so not my kind of thing. But I don't want to be negative so I ask, 'What kind of music would you want to play?'

He's into all sorts of indie bands that I've only vaguely heard of. At least it's not heavy metal, which is my least favourite. He takes out his phone and starts sending me links to some songs.

'Of course, we should really write our own stuff, but doing covers is a start.'

I'm torn between two feelings: pride that he's asking me, and nervousness that he expects me to say yes. I don't know if him saying "we" means he thinks I've already agreed to take part. I'd really like to help Jamie, but I'd probably have a panic attack before going on stage, like I nearly had at the talent show.

'You'd be lead singer, wouldn't you?' I say, not helping matters but too curious to stop myself. 'And play guitar?'

'Your voice is better.'

'I'd *hate* to be a lead singer.'

'Okay, so you'd be on backing vocals and keyboard, I'm vocals and guitar. It would be useful to have a bass player, but the really essential thing is drums. You know anyone who plays drums?'

'Nathan Jones might still play.'

'Would he suit us?'

A happy glow creeps through me when he says "us",

but I try to focus. 'I don't know him well. He's friendly with Rory and that crowd.'

'Tall, skinny boy, ginger hair?'

'That's him.'

'He might be okay. Shall I ask him or will you?'

This is all going a bit fast for me.

'Look, I can ask him for you if you want. But I don't think I can be in a band. I'm not really sure I've got time right now.'

'Oh.' I can see Jamie kind of deflate into himself. He lets out a long breath and his hand falls loosely to his side. 'Sorry, I was getting a bit carried away.'

'No. It's fine. It's a good idea. I'm just not sure I'm the right person.'

'Don't you want to think about it, at least?'

It's nice that he asked me, and the more I turn the idea over in my head, the more I think jamming with Jamie sounds quite fun. But does he know how terrible I am at performing? He'd be better off with someone confident and outgoing. I'm fed up of disappointing people.

'Not really,' I say.

Too late I realise I've already disappointed Jamie because the walk back is more subdued. To make things worse, as we head back towards my house we meet Lily walking in the opposite direction. She's probably been to visit Tom or Sarah.

There's no reason why I shouldn't be walking with Jamie, but the way she stops and stares makes me uncomfortable. 'Didn't expect to run into you two,' she says.

'We've been walking Lucy,' says Jamie, like he needs to explain. He sounds uncomfortable too. Is he embarrassed to be seen with me?

Lily raises her eyebrows. 'I didn't realise you two were so friendly.'

'Why shouldn't we be?' says Jamie.

'I just never thought ...' Lily seems to change her mind about whatever she was saying, and looks frustrated suddenly. 'Oh, look, never mind.' And she heads off down the street, leaving us staring after her.

'That was a bit abrupt,' says Jamie. He forces a laugh. 'I thought she was a friend of yours!'

'She is,' I say, although I don't even know if it's true anymore. 'Anyway, I'd better go in.' We're standing outside my house and Toby is making slight movements on his side of the fence like he's aiming for the gateway. These days you can never be sure if his movements are intentional or if he's just confused. 'Hey Tobes, have you been missing me?'

'Okay. See you around.' Jamie quickens his pace. I watch as he reaches the corner where he has to turn left. He looks right, in the direction Lily went, then pulls Lucy to heel and heads out of town towards his own house.

I take Toby inside and head up to my room, pausing in the bathroom to wash my hands because I couldn't resist cuddling Toby. Then I close the door and take out my phone. I hate this awkwardness with Lily. I want to change it. But I also hate the way she looked at Jamie and me, like she was amazed he'd spend time with me. Like she disapproved. What has it got to do with her?

I scowl at my phone, scroll past Lily, and look for Nathan Jones.

Jamie

I knew Gemma was going to be cautious about the band idea, but I still blurted it out without trying to soften her up first. It's such a shame because she'd be so good. I'm okay at singing and guitar, just like I'm okay at a lot of stuff. But she's *good*. She'd really add something to the group.

And then we had to bump into bloody Lily. Gemma looked so uncomfortable I wondered if she was embarrassed to be seen with me. Or maybe there's some girl code about hanging out with a friend's ex? I mean, yes, I broke up with Lily, but she was hardly heartbroken about it.

I realise I've spent most of the evening thinking about Gemma. Why stop there?

I pick up my phone and message her.

Jamie: I still think you'd be great in the band. Have you listened to any of those songs I sent you?

I'm not going to give up. If I can get her involved I

think we can really make something of this. Plus, I like spending time with her.

She replies.

Gemma: Not yet, I'll listen to them now.

Jamie: Awesome. Let me know what you think.

I give a sigh of relief that I haven't scared her off completely. We chat for a bit about music. It's great finding out what she likes and trying to persuade her to step out of her comfort zone. Of course, being in a band might be so far outside of her comfort zone that she might never get there. But I'm determined to give it a try.

There's a call on my phone from a number I don't recognise.

'Hello?'

'Hi, is that Jamie? It's Karl here. Karl Miller.'

'Oh. Hi.' I have absolutely no idea what this can be about. Karl was in my year at school but we were never friends.

He says hesitantly, 'Look. I've got a problem. Well, the football team have. You know, the Cuthbert Colts?'

'Oh?' The Colts are the local junior team.

'We've got a match tomorrow evening but the ref has let us down. Jock's desperate to find someone because we've already rescheduled twice. Someone said you do refereeing?'

'Er, yeah. I do.'

'So ... can you help out?'

'I'm not sure.' I still haven't switched my registration back from Glasgow. I don't know if I even want to carry on reffing. They messed me around big time. 'I'm not actually registered down here. And you can't just go and ref any match you choose.'

'Oh. Okay. Never– What …? Listen, Jock wants a word with you.'

And then the Colts' coach, Jock Skinner, is on the other end of the phone, and not half as willing to back down as Karl was.

'You're still on the referee list, aren't you? We've had refs from outside the area before, so why not you? We really need this match to go ahead.'

I can hear Karl in the background telling someone, 'He probably doesn't want to do it.'

Perversely, that makes me want to at least consider it. 'Listen. I don't know if it's possible, but I'll see what I can do, okay?'

'Well done, lad. We appreciate it.'

'I can't promise anything. I'll look online this evening but I may need to speak to an actual person, which will have to be tomorrow morning.'

'Hang on a sec while I get the match details for you. I'm sure you'll be able to sort it. I'll make contact with the Refs' Association from this side too.'

Jesus, what have I agreed to now? If it's not my mum trying to organise my life, it's random footballers finding stuff for me to do. Except … the idea of reffing a match again is appealing. I've missed it. Maybe that's part of the reason I've been feeling so down. That and the fresh humiliation of trying and failing to grasp the filing system at Dad's office. Who knows? Maybe reffing will be the one thing I get right this week.

I log on to the website and see what I need to do to make this happen.

I don't know Karl Miller well. He's Donny Miller's brother but they're not a bit alike. Good footballer, but not a social butterfly. I'd forgotten there were still people like him around town, people who hadn't gone away to uni. People who know that I had, and that I'd dropped out. Probably laughed about it …

I groan. I'm no longer so sure I want to go and ref for them now, but I've logged my availability online so I suppose I'll just have to wait and see what happens.

Apparently when someone is desperate for a ref, they can sort out the paperwork no problem.

At seven the following evening I find myself pulling on the black kit for the first time in weeks. It feels good. I check I've got all the requirements – notepad, yellow and red cards, whistle. It's going to be strange reffing a game where I'll probably know half the players on one team. I've never had any official dealings with the Cuthbert Colts, so the opposing team shouldn't be able to accuse me of bias. That doesn't mean they won't, of course.

I borrow Mum's car. She's happy enough to lend it to me for something "useful" like this. Or maybe just to get me out of the house. I get to the ground in good time and the whole match is a doddle. One of those where there are no serious fouls, where the guys on both teams are joking with each other rather than screaming, and everyone seems happy with the one-one draw.

All in all, a really easy reintroduction to refereeing.

Jock comes over at the end of the match to shake hands and thank me for helping out. Karl nods at me but doesn't come over. Which is good. I definitely don't need the other team to think I'm in cahoots with them.

On Friday I'm out at the pub having a drink with Rob, who's home for the weekend. He doesn't seem bothered one way or the other about me dropping out of uni.

'Just think, mate, no exams!' he says and that's the end of the discussion. The lack of interest is oddly reassuring.

We're on our second pint when a guy comes over who I realise is Karl Miller. He looks a bit different when he's not covered in mud from too many sliding tackles.

He gives me a slight smile. 'Just wanted to say thanks for doing the match the other night.'

'No bother. Any time. Although, actually, it's not up to me. Refs don't get to choose their matches, for obvious reasons.'

'Shame that,' he says. 'We'd definitely ask for you again. You didn't blow for every poxy little tackle.'

'You mean he was favouring the Colts? Get in!' says

Rob. 'Didn't think that was allowed.'

'It isn't. Don't be stupid.' I shut him down fast. Talk like that can easily get out of hand, and if I'm back refereeing I certainly don't want any black marks against me.

'He didn't favour anyone, unfortunately,' says Karl, and goes back to his own table, where I see some of the other Colts footballers.

'See you're making new friends now you're home,' says Rob.

'He's not really a friend.' That crowd steered well clear of me at school. Or maybe they thought I steered clear of them? I didn't, exactly, but I didn't make much of an effort either. Although I suppose not being that friendly with someone at school doesn't mean you can't be afterwards. Gemma being the perfect example.

Gemma

Rosie's still off school. I try discussing her with Mum, and even with Sarah, but we're all at a loss.

'It's not your problem, dear,' says Mum.

Sarah has other ideas. 'What does Lily think?' she asks.

Which puts me in the awkward position of not knowing what to say to her about Lily and me. Tom can't have mentioned anything.

'Lily doesn't always have the right answer.' Just saying that makes me miss Lily, even though I'm still annoyed with her. Her answers might not always be right, but she does usually have one.

'I'd like to meet Rosie,' says Sarah. 'What do you think? Would that help?'

'Maybe,' I say doubtfully. I'm not sure Rosie is up to meeting anyone new right now.

She gets dressed now apparently. That's some improvement, and it means she comes to my house for her next lesson.

'This is the first time she's been out of the house,' says Mrs Thomson in an undertone as I lead Rosie away to the music room. Both she and Rosie look thinner and paler than ever. It can't be easy being a single parent and your kid having these problems.

The lesson seems to go well. Rosie's already moved on to playing pieces that would take other people months to get to. The fingering seems to come naturally to her. We even do a bit of singing practice, because I find I am also a firm believer in being able to sing along to the music.

Afterwards Rosie wanders around the little piano room, like she wants to stay longer. She turns the pages of some of the music, and then starts looking at a cookbook I got from the library. There's no hurry because I told her mum I'd walk her home.

'What's this?' she asks, opening it so she can see the beautiful photos. I wonder why the food I make never looks like that.

'Recipe book.'

'I can see that.' From another kid that might be cheeky, but Rosie's tone is flat.

I reach for the book and start leafing through it myself. 'I thought I might become vegetarian.'

'Mum and I don't each much meat.'

I wonder if money is an issue for them – meat isn't cheap. Then I feel guilty because they're paying me for the piano lessons. What if they can't really afford it? As far as I can tell, Mrs Thomson only works part-time. Should I offer to carry on teaching Rosie for free?

I chew my lip. Somehow I've gone from not wanting to teach Rosie even for money, to being willing to do it for free.

I say, 'Have you thought any more about extra lessons? Maybe a short one later in the week? No charge.' I can't think of a way to refuse payment for the main lesson without making a big thing of it.

Rosie lets the book fall shut and picks up her coat. 'I should go home now.'

'What's wrong?'

She shrugs and says, almost inaudibly, 'Mum says you don't have time.'

A lot has changed since I told Mrs Thomson that, but all I say is, 'You're a quick learner so I don't have to do that much preparation for your lessons. And I thought you might be a bit bored being at home so much. It was just a thought.' One I'll have to make sure Mrs Marshall doesn't hear about. She can't understand why I won't take on her proposed second pupil.

Rosie mumbles something.

'Huh?'

'I don't want to be any trouble.'

'I like teaching you music. I think it's good for me.' And as I say it, I realise it's true. Having to break things down and explain them makes such a difference to how I understand my own playing.

Rosie looks at me doubtfully. 'Thank you. I think I should go home now.'

For the moment I leave it at that. I know how it feels to be pushed when I'm feeling shy and unsure. I just wish I knew whether that's Rosie's only problem.

Gemma

Nathan seems keen on joining Jamie's band. I give him Jamie's contact details and I let Jamie know he'll be in touch. I feel quite proud of myself for being so proactive.

Jamie replies.

Jamie: Thanks! I'll invite him round.

After a couple of minutes, he adds:

Jamie: Be good if you came along too.

Being in a band has never been something I wanted to do, but … neither was teaching Rosie, and that's been really good for me, hasn't it? And, okay, maybe I am enjoying it too.

Gemma: I'll see.

I say, which means I don't have to make a decision right now.

A couple of days later Nathan comes up to me at lunchtime. 'Jamie Abernethy wants me to go round to his house, but I'm really not sure.'

For goodness sake, I thought I was supposed to be the indecisive one! 'Why not?'

'You know, being in a band with *him.*' He shifts his feet. 'Bit of a prick, isn't he? All up himself.'

'No he's not!' I don't think Jamie ever was like that, really. And this year he's even less so. I say, 'He's a nice guy, who wants to start a band and needs a drummer. You should give it a try.'

Nathan rubs his freckled forehead. 'It's just, like, I don't really know him.'

He looks down in a way that reminds me of Rosie. Maybe that's why I say, 'Look, if it helps, I'll come along with you. Jamie did mention something about needing a keyboard player. I don't really have the time right now but ...'

'That'd be great.' Nathan gives a smile of relief. 'It's after school tomorrow, is that okay? He lives in one of those huge houses on the edge of town. I've never been to one before.'

'At least there's bound to be room for the band to practise without annoying the neighbours.' Why am I the one being so positive about this? I just don't want Jamie to be disappointed. I get the impression he's been quite down about the whole dropping out of uni thing.

I say goodbye to Nathan and go sit with Donny and Tom – and of course Lily. Our year's too small for me to avoid her completely, and why should I?

It's Lily who says, 'Nice that you've suddenly got all these boys running after you.'

'Ha ha.' I wouldn't rate Nathan any higher on the attraction stakes than me. He's too tall and skinny.

'Is Nathan going to be in Jamie's band?' asks Tom. I've told him all about it. He and Sarah think I should get involved too.

'He's considering it.'

'And you?'

'Probably not,' I say. Then I realise Lily is still listening and I don't want her to think I'm pathetic, like this is yet another thing I'm not doing because I'm scared. I say, 'But I'm going to Jamie's with Nathan so ... we'll see ...'

Jamie

Things are looking up a bit. I've got into the swing of being a clerical assistant and no longer make a fool of myself ten times every morning. Mum is so pleased I'm "doing something useful" that she's stopped getting on at me so much. I've reffed another game in Kirkdouglas and I've got one coming up in Dumfries. And Nathan Jones is coming round this afternoon to see if he wants to be in a band with me.

The last thing I expect is for him to turn up with Gemma in tow.

'You came! That's great.'

She actually blushes, the colour flooding her pale skin.

'I came to show Nathan where you live,' she says, but that can't be the real reason. Our house is hard to miss. Is there something going on between them? Is that why Gemma knew that Nathan played drums? Why am I such an idiot that I have never once wondered if she has a boyfriend?

'Well, come in,' I say, less enthusiastic.

I take them across to the old garage which no one uses now because Dad's had a new double one built. It has got a radiator in it so it's not freezing cold, but the floor is plain concrete. It's going to be the perfect band-practice room.

'Wow, you've got Pearl drums,' says Nathan. '*And* Sabien cymbals. Cool.'

'My brother Michael learnt for a while and we never got round to selling them when he quit. I don't know if they're any good.'

Nathan has folded himself onto the little stool behind the drums and started adjusting them. I pass him a set of sticks and within minutes he's trying out rhythms, adjusting the cymbals, trying them again.

'You're good,' I say. I'm watching Gemma, who is watching him too. If she only came to show Nathan the way here, she doesn't need to stay. The fact that she is either means that she likes him, or that she's reconsidering being in the band. Part of me hopes she just wants to spend time with me.

'I'm okay,' Nathan replies, playing a fill and then a rock groove. 'This is a good set-up. You could do with a replacement hi-hat, but the rest's okay. I won't need to bring my kit over.'

And just like that, I have a drummer. But I'm still wondering about Gemma. I've got a keyboard set up because I've been messing around on it myself, but for now I just pick up the guitar.

'Let's try something,' I say to Nathan.

'Okay. Any ideas?'

Gemma takes a seat on the tatty armchair and listens as we suggest everything from Ed Sheeran to Rabbie Burns.

'It doesn't matter what you do to begin with,' she says eventually. 'You just need to see if you can play together, get the feel for each other musically.'

'Let's do 'Ace Of Spades',' I say.

'Gah!' Gemma throws her hands wide. 'I thought you were going to do indie, not heavy metal.'

"Ace Of Spades' is 'Ace Of Spades',' I say. It's not just a genre, it's bigger than that.

Nathan nods. He gets it.

We have a go and, after a few false starts, manage a pretty good run through. Having drums backing you makes a huge difference. The sound is bigger, more confident. I get really into yelling the lyrics, even though it's only the three of us in a garage.

'Cool,' says Nathan when we finish.

'Not bad,' says Gemma, narrowing her eyes. 'But you'll ruin your voice if you go on shouting like that. And you weren't quite in sync. And the drums did kind of overpower the sound of the guitar.'

I grin at her. I'm feeling a bit high from the singing, and now she's handed me this on a plate.

'That's why we need something else to hold the melody. Like, you know, the keyboard.'

She scrunches up her nose. 'That is not what I was suggesting.'

'No, but you know it makes sense. And you've just shown how useful your music knowledge can be. You understand this better than we do.'

'I don't really.' Nevertheless she stands up and wanders over to the keyboard, like she can't stop herself. She picks out a tune and pulls a face. 'This doesn't sound right. I told you, I've never played keyboard before.'

'I've been messing around with the settings, that's why. You'll pick it up no bother.' I go over and change it back to ordinary keyboard. 'I can show you more later, but really, for someone like you there's not much to it.'

She picks out another song, one-handed. Her playing is quick and light.

'Be good if there were three of us playing,' says Nathan.

I don't know what his motivation is for saying that, but I decide to worry over it later and concentrate on keeping Gemma involved right now. 'What shall we play?'

'I am not doing 'Ace Of Spades'.'

'Okay, you choose. But nothing classical.'

Eventually we agree on 'All Star' by Smash Mouth, because we all at least know the chorus. I call it up on my laptop and we try it a few times. Each time is better than the last. Nathans's a solid drummer. Gemma's playing starts off a bit too precise and perfect, but gradually she loosens up. By the final time I don't need to look at the words to the verses.

'Nailed it!' I say. 'That was a laugh. We're going to be great.'

'Aye, you can tell that after doing just one cover,' says Gemma, but she's grinning.

I say to Nathan, 'Shall we meet again at the weekend, work out what stuff we really want to play?'

'Cool.'

'Okay with you Gemma?'

She pauses, eyes narrowed, but she's hooked. I can tell she is. 'I suppose I could manage Saturday afternoon.'

Yes!

Gemma

I'm sitting chatting to Sarah in her bedroom. One of the few pluses about not spending time with Lily (and by extension Tom), is that I've been hanging out with Sarah more.

'You're going to be in a band with Jamie Abernethy?' she says. 'That's so cool!'

I shake my head. 'Stupid, more like.'

Sarah looks at me consideringly, head to one side. 'You seem to have been seeing quite a bit of Jamie.'

'Not really. Sometimes we happen to walk our dogs together.'

'And now you're in his band.'

'He asked me to help him find a drummer 'cause he knows I do music. It's nothing.'

The way she's looking at me makes me feel uncomfortable. She must realise that because all she says is, 'And is Jamie playing guitar? I hope he's better than Tom when he accompanied you at the talent show.'

'Tom was fine,' I say. Although, obviously, Jamie is loads better. And Jamie's so into it, sometimes it's hard not to get distracted watching him.

Sarah grins as my cheeks turn pink of their own accord. Time to change the subject.

'I'm still worried about Rosie,' I say, which isn't a lie. It's so easy to see myself in her painful shyness and she's on my mind a lot. I pull around the tail of my plait. I fiddle with it, which is better than chewing it. 'She's refusing to go to school and she doesn't seem to have any friends.'

'Is she ill?'

'I don't know. I don't think so. She's very thin, but then so's her mum. I think she's just incredibly shy.'

'Even with you? You've been teaching her for ages.'

'Sometimes she seems to be getting a bit more comfortable around me, and then she clams up again.'

I find I'm chewing my hair after all and for the moment I let myself. It helps me think. 'I feel so sorry for her. I know what it's like to be so shy, but at least I had you and Tom.' *And Lily*, I add silently. She made such an effort to be friends with me back when I barely spoke that eventually I had no choice but to be her friend back. What on earth would I be like if Lily hadn't brought me even this far out of my shell?

'So what are you going to do?' Sarah interrupts my thoughts.

I toss my plait back over my shoulder. 'The Easter holidays start on Friday. I'll tell Mrs Thomson that

Rosie can stay at my house while she's at work. If I spend more time with her, maybe I'll work something out.'

'But do you want a kid hanging around you all day every day for a fortnight?'

'It won't be every day. Her mum only works part-time. And it won't be just me. I'll definitely introduce you to her while she's with me. I might even invite Lily round.' I won't, of course, but I need to pretend things are okay.

'And Jamie Abernethy?' says Sarah with a smirk, bringing the conversation back to where it started.

'Why would I involve Jamie Abernethy?'

Sarah just laughs in answer.

Jamie

Gemma and Nathan come over on Saturday. Nathan doesn't say much but he has a couple of suggestions for songs we can try. Our choices are all over the place, from rock to country to techno, but hopefully we'll eventually find our own style.

Afterwards I have the excellent idea that Gemma should stay on so I can show her more settings on the keyboard. Nathan grins at her as he gets up to go and she scowls in return. She's been quite relaxed and chatty while he's there, but immediately she seems quieter. Nervous, even.

'You okay?' I say.

'Yeah, fine.'

I show her all the keyboard settings I know, and we have a bit of fun playing a Calvin Harris track with an organ set up, and then 'The Bonnie Bonnie Banks of Loch Lomond' on synth. But still I feel there's something off with her, like she doesn't want to be here, or to be sitting so close to me. She keeps checking her watch.

'Look, if you need to be somewhere else we can finish now.'

'No. Yeah. Well, okay.'

She gets up and moves away.

'Sorry. I didn't mean to keep you. You obviously wanted to head off with Nathan.'

'Not particularly.'

'So …?' I'm put out. Until now Gemma has been the one person I could be totally relaxed around; the one person who seemed to like spending time with me and expected nothing back. 'If you don't want to be here or do this band thing, it's fine, no pressure.'

'It's not that. It's just.' She squeezes her hands together. 'Look, this is going to sound stupid. Don't take it the wrong way, okay? It's just that people are saying you and I spend a lot of time together and there must be something going on between us. First it was Tom's sister Sarah, and then Nathan said something on our way here. It's kind of getting to me …'

I stare at her. 'So, what, they think a girl and a guy can't just be friends, is that it?'

She gives a sigh of relief. 'Exactly. And of course they can. It's just that people can be so stupid about it. I didn't want you to think that *I* think that, because one or two people are making comments and … well, you know.'

She's not explaining herself very clearly, but I get that she doesn't want people thinking we're together.

Which for some reason pisses me off.

'Is there something going on between you and Nathan?' I ask.

'No!'

'Well, that's good …' I trail off. I study her properly. She's wearing a dress over dark leggings, no make-up, her beautiful hair pinned up on her head. She's tiny, and right now she looks like an angry fairy.

'What? Stop staring!' A faint colour comes to her pale cheeks.

'I'm not staring! I can look at you, can't I?'

She takes another step back. I really don't think she introduced this topic on purpose, but her bringing it up makes me wonder – do I *want* to be just friends with her? Or would I prefer something more?

Gemma says, 'I'm going now,' grabs her coat and bag and leaves. Like she's afraid I'll make a move on her or something. I'm wondering why I didn't. Not make a move, exactly, but try to get her to stay. Hold her hand. See if there's more there. Because now that's something I really want to find out.

Gemma

I run the conversation over again in my head but it still seems weird. Maybe it seemed weird to Jamie too, and that's why he looked so completely nonplussed. Why did I have to open my big mouth?

Everything was fine when we were just meeting up naturally, with no one else around or knowing. No one commenting. Now when I see Jamie there are other people's questions in my head making me feel awkward. What if he starts feeling awkward too? It's going to spoil everything. And for what?

Jamie Abernethy would never be interested in me that way. I *know* that and yet … and yet I can't help thinking about the way his eyes rested on me for so long. How standing close to him at the keyboard made me feel hot all over. And the way he looked at me when I told him people thought we were together.

But that doesn't mean he's interested in me. I probably just made him feel awkward. I cringe at the thought. I should avoid him for a while. Hopefully he'll just forget about this. Maybe if I keep myself busy enough, I will too.

Fast forward to Thursday and really, I don't know what's happening to me. I thought making my own decisions would mean doing fewer things I didn't like. It doesn't seem to be working out that way.

At the end of registration, Mr Barrett, the Deputy Rector, comes in. 'I just wanted a word with you all. As you know there'll be no lessons for Sixth Years the first week after the Easter holidays. It's a new experiment this year to give you time to explore opportunities, get some work experience.'

'Or study, since we do have our exams coming up *very soon*,' says Lily. She's said from the start that the timing is ridiculous – perhaps because they didn't consult her about it beforehand.

'You'll have had two whole weeks of the standard Easter holidays to study,' Mr Barrett says cheerfully. 'Now, for those of you who want a placement but haven't got one yet, we've had another couple of offers come in. The local primary school have said they're willing to take three students instead of two, and the hydroelectric place have agreed to take someone, and ...'

So far I've been very successful at avoiding committing to any of these work placements. People haven't even pushed me much because they all think I'm so committed to my music that I don't need to try out anything else. But if I'm going to help Rosie, and I do want to, then maybe this is my chance.

I raise my hand. 'I might be interested in doing the primary school placement.'

He makes a note on his clipboard. 'Excellent. Thank you, Gemma. Anyone else?'

Oh god, I can't believe I just did that. Nor can Lily by the looks of it. Which is probably the only reason why I don't seize Mr Barrett's clipboard and cross my name right back out.

Jamie

It's the first week of the Easter holidays and I haven't seen Gemma since that strange conversation after band practice. Nathan and I have had another couple of practice sessions, but the first time Gemma couldn't come because she had some family thing on, and the next she was babysitting. We haven't been for a walk together in ages either. I miss her smiles and the way everything she says seems thoughtful and considered.

I try to arrange a session for the following afternoon, but she says she's babysitting again. I get the feeling she's avoiding me.

Jamie: Who is this kid you're looking after, anyway?

Gemma: She's called Rosie. I've been teaching her piano.

Jamie: If she's learning piano, you could bring her along with you. Be good for her to see you playing keyboard.

There's a pause, which makes me hopeful. Then:

Gemma: I'm not sure. She's only 10 and she's quite shy.

I feel frustrated. I wish I knew if this was a real reason or an excuse. I want to see Gemma again and I don't care if she has some kid in tow or not.

Enough beating around the bush.

Jamie: Look, if you're just making excuses not to see me, say so.

I toss my phone on the table, determined not to just stare at it until she replies. I start doing the washing up that Mum has been moaning about. We have a dishwasher but she doesn't like to put pans into it, or glasses, or half her fancy cutlery. Bloody Mum. My hands are wrist-deep in soapy water when the phone eventually gives a beep.

Gemma: Rosie says she'd like to see a real band practice even though I told her it's not that exciting. What time should we be there?

She's agreed! Not enthusiastically, or even particularly willingly, but I can live with that. I'm seeing Gemma again tomorrow.

I attach my phone to the portable speaker and go back to washing up. I'm in such a good mood I dry the pots and put them away and then wipe down all the surfaces. I am a perfect son.

Mum's well pleased when she gets home. Dad says, 'Is there something you want?'

'Just to keep on using the old garage as a practice room for the band.'

'A band wasn't really what I was hoping you'd be spending your spare time on,' says Mum.

'It's fine by me, just as long as we can't hear you in the house,' says Dad. 'It's good you're keeping busy.'

And it's true, I am fairly busy, with refereeing and the clerical work and now the band. It's just my social life that needs some improvement, and I've got one or two ideas about that.

Gemma

I feel nervous going back to Jamie's. I'm glad I've got Rosie with me, like she's some kind of shield. And she seems okay about the whole thing. I was worried it was going to stress her out.

The only thing she says on the walk there is, 'I've never met anyone in a band.'

'It's not a real band,' I say, then feel bad for belittling Jamie's idea. 'I mean, it *is* a band, but we're just starting up.'

We reach Jamie's house and both pause. It really is an impressive place. Double-fronted, white-painted, with a fancy red-tiled roof that sweeps up and down at heights. The garden is massive, too, meaning the house is set well back from the road.

When I came here with Nathan we knocked on the front door and Jamie took us across to the separate garage/music room. I can see a car in the driveway which I think is Jamie's mum's. I don't want to knock on the door and have to speak to her. She's tall and glamorous and scary.

To my relief, I hear a drum roll from across the garden. Nathan and Jamie must already be in the garage.

I take Rosie's hand. 'Come on. It's this way.'

The practice is okay. Rosie sits near me and watches and doesn't say a word. Jamie and Nathan have been working on a couple of covers and once Jamie gets the music up for me on his laptop, I can join in fairly well. We haven't gelled yet, but I kind of like the sound we make. We try an Arctic Monkeys cover, and then Kasabian (*not* my choice). Nathan is really good on the drums, better than I expected, and Jamie's guitar and singing are great.

And everything is normal between Jamie and me. He doesn't look at me in a different way, we just talk about the music and timings. I'm relieved and disappointed.

We add 'Heart Heart' by Withered Hand to our repertoire and it goes really well. As we're packing up, Nathan says, 'I know someone who wants to join the band. If you still think we need a bass player?'

'Who?' Jamie and I ask at the same time. Apparently I've gone from not wanting to be in this band to being protective about who else is allowed to join.

'Erin Seaton.'

Erin is a studious girl in our year. Just about the last person I'd expect to play bass guitar. But I kind of like the idea of another girl in the band.

'Quiet girl with glasses?' says Jamie, frowning.

'I didn't know she played any instruments,' I say.

'Apparently she taught herself. She does stuff like that.'

'You know her well?' Jamie, like me, seems unsure he wants to let someone else into our group.

'She's my cousin,' says Nathan.

'Is she any good?' asks Jamie.

'Don't know.'

'We should give her a try,' I say, so firmly that they both turn to stare at me. 'All the songs we've done so far have a bass line that we're missing.'

'What's this girl like?' Jamie addresses the question to me, even though she's Nathan's cousin.

'I don't know her that well. She's more into sciences so she's not been in many of my classes. But she always seems nice.'

'Okay. Nathan can ask her to come along to the next practice and we'll see. We all need to agree.'

'Seems fair,' says Nathan.

We agree on a time for the next practice and then Rosie and I head off because I need to get her home. As we leave, Jamie looks at me thoughtfully. My heart gives a stupid little skip. 'See you at the next practice, then,' is all he says.

He doesn't suggest walking the dogs or meeting up in between. I nod and hope I don't look disappointed.

'Did you enjoy that?' I ask Rosie as we head back to her house. I'd forgotten she was there half the time. She was still and silent, and I got caught up in the music and then the discussion about Erin. She's looking at her feet. I hope the whole thing hasn't set her back just when she's started to seem a little happier. I even got Sarah to walk into town with us once to get ice creams and Rosie didn't seem to mind. I'm really hoping whatever she's struggling with will just blow over and she'll be willing to go back to school when the new term starts.

'You have nice friends,' she says softly.

I'm not sure either Jamie or Nathan spoke to her, apart from saying hi, so I don't know what she bases that on, but I'm pleased all the same.

Jamie

I'm not making any progress with Gemma. It's clear that she's avoiding me. I've suggested a couple of things we could do together but she's never free, and I don't want to suggest something else in case it pushes her to say no for good.

I used to think Gemma Anderson was a little mouse, maybe even a bit of pushover – how else had she managed to stay friends with Lily all this time? Now I realise that's not the case at all. Apparently once she decides against something, she's hard to move. And I'm afraid she's decided against spending time alone with me.

But I don't want to give up. Since Gemma doesn't want to walk Lucy with me, I take her for a run, trying and failing to come up with a plan of action. Then, during the cool down, I get a message from Lily of all people. She's having a party on Saturday and do I want to come along? Yes, I bloody do! Gemma's bound to be there, without any ten-year-olds in tow. And I haven't been to a party in months. Lily used to throw really good ones.

Of course, I haven't thought it through at all. At first glance most of the people there seem to be from Lily's year. People I know slightly but never really socialised with, even when she and I were going out. They all seem so young, excited just to have access to alcohol. Plus I feel like they're watching me, secretly pleased that I'm not the success I pretended to be because I've dropped out of uni. Making a move on Gemma in this setting is just not going to happen.

I'm tempted to turn round and head right back out, but that would be running away. Instead, I go to the kitchen to grab a beer and find that there are some guys there I know. Mark is someone from my year who I always kind of envied because he was in a band. And I recognise the guy he's talking to as Karl Miller. I seem to be bumping into him quite a bit these days.

'Hiya,' he says, and shifts so I can join their circle.

We chat for a while. Then Lily comes into the room and shouts, 'Enough talk about football. It's time to dance!' She ushers us all into the massive living/dining room. All the furniture has been pushed back, so I know she means business, but I manage to edge my way out of the crowd she's herding.

I'm about to head back to the safety of the kitchen when I see Gemma sitting on one of the settees along the wall. There are three other people squashed up beside her, but they're talking to each other rather than to her. I can't resist.

I cross the room and perch on the armrest, bending down to shout above the noise. 'How you doing?'

'Fine.'

I don't know how the others are managing a conversation. Donny Miller has turned the music right up and it's deafening. It's easier to not even try and talk. So I just sit there, close to Gemma, my arm balanced on the back of the settee to stop me falling off, sipping my beer. I start to relax.

When there's a break in the music, I say to Gemma, 'Want to dance?'

She looks down. 'Not really.'

Then the song starts, and it's 'Heart Heart'.

'Come on, we've got to dance to this!' I take her hand and pull her to her feet and she comes not too unwillingly.

The song has a great beat. I'm not really a dancer, but anyone can enjoy this. I know the song so well now, I join in the chorus with the others. Gemma smiles. Her movements are contained, no leaping and throwing out her arms like some of the others, but she's completely in time with the music. She's wearing a short, long-sleeved black dress with black tights, no colour at all except for her hair, which she has pinned up again. She looks other-worldly, lost in her thoughts and the music, even when the others are shouting the words. Then she looks up and sees me watching her, and blushes.

As soon as the music stops she says, 'I need another drink,' and heads for the kitchen.

I follow her, because I don't want to be separated yet. And I hate the idea she's trying to get away from me. We find Nathan in the kitchen, which is useful. We can talk about the band (which we *really* need to find a name for) and I tell them about a song I've been writing. It'll be our first original piece. *If* they like it. *If* it's any good.

'Sounds great,' says Nathan, who's definitely chattier after a beer or two. 'If you message us a clip, we can look at it before the next practice session.'

'I haven't got very far.'

'Send us what you've got, I'd like to have a go. Pity we're back to school again on Monday.'

Gemma sighs. 'And I'm not even back at *our* school. I'm doing this work experience thing in the primary. I must be mad.'

I say, 'I didn't know you were interested in primary teaching.'

'I'm not. I just had this stupid idea that maybe I could help Rosie.'

'Why do you need to help Rosie?'

Gemma shrugs. Her hair is falling down, a splash of red against the pale skin of her shoulders. 'I don't know. She's not happy at school.'

'Join the club,' says Nathan.

She shakes her head at him. 'No, it's more than just normal not really liking school. I'm worried about her.'

'Shouldn't her parents be worrying about her?' I don't see why Gemma should take on this responsibility.

'They are. Well, her mum is. Her dad doesn't seem to be around.'

'So it's not your problem.'

'Just because it's not my problem doesn't mean I shouldn't try to help.' She frowns. 'Oh, god, am I starting to sound like Lily?'

'Yes,' says Nathan grinning.

'No,' I say, impressed. 'You're just being kind.'

'I don't know about that. Anyway, I think I have helped a bit. She says she'll go back to school on Monday because I told her I'd be there too. Now I'm going to have to go in early and see the head teacher and ask if I can be with Rosie's class.' She bites her lip. 'No, I'm really not like Lily. She'd do that without batting an eyelid, but I hate having to go and speak to people.'

'Get Lily to do it for you,' says Nathan. 'She won't mind.'

Gemma glares. 'No. I'm going to do it. This is my thing.'

I want to tell her that I admire what she's doing. But Donny and a group of his friends have come in and our conversation gets lost in the noise. By the time things have sorted themselves out, Gemma has managed to sneak away.

After a while I head back to the main room. It's full of flailing, sweaty people, but no sign of Gemma. There's a door open at the far end and I go through that to where I remember there's a conservatory. There are no lights on in here so it's presumably supposed to be off limits. By the faint light of the moon I can see Gemma standing at the far windows, staring out into the shadowy garden.

'Hey,' I say softly. 'You okay?'

She glances over her shoulder and then turns back. 'Of course. It was just a bit too noisy in there. And hot.' I go and stand beside her and she gestures at her woollen dress. 'I don't think I chose the right clothes.'

I touch her arm. 'I like it.'

'It's just a dress.'

Someone crashes into the glass door, banging it shut. It's hard to be sure but I think it might be Lily. It's certainly her shriek of laughter I hear, followed by the deeper voice of a guy.

Gemma takes a step away from the noise. I move with her. I put up a hand to touch her hair, like I've wanted to do for days now. It's soft and very fine. Then I stroke her cheek. She looks up at me. I touch her pale lips with mine. No lipstick. She tastes of Gemma. Heaven. I think she's kissing me back and I make a move to pull her closer.

She jumps away, banging the window with her elbow.

I say. 'Sorry, I ...'

'No, no, it's fine. I've got to go.'

She turns and runs. It's the first time a girl's ever done that after I've kissed her. I stare after her, wanting to follow but not wanting to upset her more. Because clearly I have upset her. Why did I move in like that? Just because I've been fancying her like mad all evening doesn't mean she fancies me back. I sometimes think there's an answering spark, but now is not one of those times. I am such an idiot.

I give her five minutes to cool down and then go to look for her. I can't find her anywhere. Eventually I hear someone say she had a headache and went home.

Brilliant. Just brilliant.

There's nothing for me at the party now, but I still hang around. I don't know if I'm pretending to enjoy it for my own sake or because I want to show others that I still fit in. At the end of the evening I find myself helping Tom and some girls collect up the bottles and cans.

Lily comes into the kitchen when I'm shaking open yet another black bag. 'Hi you,' she says, standing between me and the door. She's had a bit to drink, but she doesn't seem too drunk.

'Hi you,' I say. I realise I haven't actually said hello to her all evening. Which is pretty bad manners, seeing as it's her party.

She frowns at me. 'Jamie, did you do something to upset Gemma?'

'Why?'

'Because she left suddenly. Said she had a headache, but I'm not sure that was true. And before that she was in the conservatory with you.'

'So?'

She studies me, eyes narrowed. 'So I don't think you should mess Gemma around. I feel like you're using her just because you haven't got any other friends here.'

Now it's my turn to stare. How could she say that? How could she even *think* that? 'You don't know what you're talking about,' I spit out.

'I just don't want her to be–'

I turn and walk out before she can finish. I'm fuming. So Lily thinks I use people, does she? She thinks there's no way I could be seriously interested in Gemma? She's just so bloody wrong.

The problem is, if she thinks that, then Gemma almost certainly thinks it too. And with support like this from Lily, what chance do I have of convincing her otherwise?

Gemma

I am such an idiot. I only went to Lily's party because it would've looked odd if I didn't. And then Jamie was there. And then we were alone in the conservatory. And then he kissed me. *Why* did he kiss me? Aargh, and why did I run away?

I was just so shocked. I bet he was too. It must have been a moment of complete madness for him. He'd had a few beers but ... but I don't think he was drunk. But why else would he kiss me? Plain, skinny, ginger Gemma.

I'm lying on my bed with the light off, pretending I'm suffering from the headache I told Mum I had when I got home. She was all sympathetic and only asked twice if I'd had too much to drink. I don't think I had. And anyway, the shock of Jamie Abernethy's lips on mine, soft and warm – well, that would have been enough to sober me up.

I picture Jamie standing in the dark conservatory beside me, hot from the dancing, his hair longer than ever and a bit wild. I couldn't see his expression. That's probably a good thing.

I groan and bury my head in the pillow. The first time a boy I really like kisses me and all I do is stand there like a statue, before legging it like an Olympian. Hopefully I can avoid him forever and everything will be fine. Except then I'll never see him again.

Another groan.

It's a long, long time before I fall asleep.

The next morning I get up early to let Toby out, because Mum and Dad usually sleep in on a Sunday. He staggers out to do his business and then barks to be let back in. He comes and leans against me where I'm sitting on the bench at the kitchen table, sipping my tea. His weight feels comforting.

I put one hand on his head and with the other I turn my phone on. It's been off since last night but I can't delay forever. It buzzes. Then buzzes again. Then a couple more times.

There's one message from Lily, so I read that first.

Lily: You OK? Did Jamie say something to upset you?

Why would she think that? Did she see what happened?

After that there are three messages from Jamie himself. I take a deep breath before opening them.

Jamie: Sorry, I didn't mean to upset you.

Jamie: Lily said you had a headache. I hope it's not too bad.

**Jamie: I'm really sorry Gemma. Just message me
so I know you're OK.**

I don't know why he's apologising. I'm the idiot who
spoilt everything.

I try about ten different replies and eventually send:
**Gemma: Still got a bit of a headache but otherwise
fine. Hope you enjoyed the rest of the party.**

There. That's nice and neutral, isn't it? Maybe he
got off with some other girl and had a brilliant time
after I left. I wish I was a nice enough person to
genuinely hope so.

I'm practising piano in the late afternoon when Lily
turns up. She has to choose *now* to come and see me?

'So you *are* alive,' she says. Mum's told her to come
straight through to the music room. She slumps down
on the floor with her back to the radiator, like she was
here just yesterday. 'Ugh. I feel like crap.'

'Of course I'm alive. Sorry I didn't reply to your
message. I ...' But I can't come up with any plausible
explanation, so I play a couple of chords instead.

She looks around the room. 'It's nice to be back
here.'

That feels like an olive branch, like she's saying
she's missed me.

Then she says, 'Gemma, what happened last night?'

'Nothing.' I'm immediately wary.

'Was it Jamie?' When I don't answer, she continues,
'I feel like it's my fault you've ended up spending so

much time with him, because you and I haven't been, you know … He must have done something to make you leave like that. What was it?'

I don't mean to respond, but I'm annoyed that she thinks everything is about her. This was about Jamie, and me. 'He kissed me.'

She jerks upright. 'Oh Gem, I'm so sorry. The bastard.'

I swing round on the piano stool so I can face her. 'Why is he a bastard?'

'Well, he obviously upset you …'

'He *surprised* me, that's all. Anyway, I messed the whole thing up as usual. I was so shocked I just left.'

'Maybe that was for the best,' says Lily. 'Look, I'm not saying that Jamie doesn't have his good points, but I don't want you to get hurt, Gem. You're so kind and all his friends are away. I worry he's taking advantage.'

The assumption that Jamie would never really be interested in me, that he's only spending time with me because there's no one better, is infuriating. It doesn't help that I've been thinking those things myself.

I say, 'Just forget it, okay?'

'If I'd known he kissed you I'd have spoke–'

'There's no need for you to speak to anyone!' I stand up. 'If you've come here to interfere then you shouldn't have bothered.' I'd actually thought she was on the point of apologising. But no, she's just so sure that I'm making a mess of my life again that she's come here to fix it.

'Gemma–'

'Lily, just stop interfering, okay? And I really do have a headache. I'm going to lie down.'

Before Lily can say more, I hustle her to the front door and see her out. I hate that Lily and I are like this right now. But I also hate that she still thinks she knows what's best for me.

I'm starting to think social media bans might be quite a good thing. I've had my phone switched off for twenty-four hours now and I'm feeling much less stressed – and that's despite having gone to see the primary school head at the crack of dawn, and shadowing the teacher in Rosie's class all day. Those things aren't actually as difficult as working out what to say to Jamie when he messages again. Or, worse, finding out that he hasn't messaged me again and doesn't want to talk at all.

I'd offered to walk home with Rosie, but her mum wanted to do it herself as it was her first day back at school. It's a good thing because in the end it's half-past four by the time the teacher, Miss Reynolds, sets me free. I hurry to the gate, adjusting my scarf so I don't get any draughts down my neck. It might be April but there's no sign of spring weather yet. I almost bump into Jamie, who's leaning against one of the gate posts.

'Ah! Jesus, what are you doing here?'

'Waiting for you. Do you know how annoying it is

when someone has their phone switched off?'

'Er, is my phone switched off?' I start walking towards my house.

He falls into step beside me. 'It is. But I remembered you said you were doing work experience here, so I thought I'd catch you when you finished. I've been waiting ages.'

'You didn't have to.'

'It was the only way I could think of to see you. Although I'd just about given up, school finished ages ago. What on earth have you been doing?'

'Helping set up project work for tomorrow,' I say, but my thoughts are really on why he wants to see me. It makes my heart beat a bit faster, the idea of him waiting there all that time just to see me.

'So,' he says after a long pause. It's starting to rain and he pulls out a beanie hat and pulls it on. Even with his hair mostly hidden and a few days' growth of beard, he looks completely gorgeous. It must be amazing to be like that. He never even seems to have spots.

I look away and speed up, even though it makes me breathless.

'Look, I just wanted you to know I'm sorry. About Saturday. I shouldn't have kissed you, at least not without asking. I don't know why I did that.'

I don't know why I did that. The words reverberate in my mind. He wishes he hadn't kissed me. Which I knew all along, so why does it still hurt?

'It's fine.'

From the corner of my eye I can see him watching me. He says, 'So, we're still friends, right?'

'I guess.'

'And you're still in the band? It's been coming together so well, it'd be a shame if you dropped out.'

Now I know what this is about. He doesn't want anything to mess up his precious band.

'Yes, I'm still in the band. I'll be at the practice on Wednesday. I'll make sure I keep my phone on in case there are any changes. And look, you don't need to walk with me. It's taking you out of your way. I'll see you on Wednesday, okay? Bye!'

He looks baffled. I probably sound a bit manic, but I just need to get away from him. He doesn't follow me any farther, but I can feel his eyes on my back until I turn the corner.

Jamie

I can't work Gemma Anderson out at all. I'm going to stop trying. I've got a referee refresher session this evening and I'm in charge of an amateur match tomorrow. That and the fascinating work at Dad's practice will keep me busy. And I'll see Gemma again at band practice on Wednesday. *If* she turns up.

The football match is between Kirkdouglas and a Dumfries team, played on the Kirkdouglas ground which is handy for me. It also seems to be handy for some of the Cuthbert Colts players, who I see watching from the sidelines. Either they're football mad or they're checking out future opposition. Or both.

Karl Miller is one of those watching and he comes over to me at the end. 'No a bad game, hey?'

'I've reffed worse.'

'We're heading over to the Newton Arms for a pint. Want to join us?'

'I need to get home and file my match report.' Even though this is only a junior game, the league still takes the whole thing seriously. My report needs to be in tonight. The last thing I want to do is get in the RA's bad books again. I know now that I really miss refereeing when I'm not doing it.

'Your report won't take that long, will it? Come and join us after if you want.'

I make a noncommittal noise and watch as he and his mates cram themselves into his souped-up Mini. It was nice of him to invite me. Surprising, too. I hardly know his crowd. On the other hand, if I don't go, I'll be stuck at home with Mum and Dad. Again.

Decision made, I head back out once the report is filed. I get myself a pint and head over to the table where Karl and his friends are sitting. I recognise Callum Ritchie from a couple of years above me, and Kieran Burns who's mostly known for being a great footballer when he's not totally radge. I pull up a stool next to Karl and listen while they dissect the game they've just watched.

'And the ref was a right eejit,' says Karl, straight-faced. 'Couldnae see a foul when he was two foot away.'

Callum glances at me. 'Aye, and that shoulda been a penalty at the start of the second half, for sure.'

I take a swallow of beer and say, 'I think what you guys need is a wee lesson in the Laws of the Game.'

I grin as they all howl with laughter. One of our PE teachers at school had gone on endlessly about "wee

196

lessons in the Laws of the Game". He was the one who got me into reffing in the first place.

'Aye. Like it's not an off-side if the player isn't active, but how the hell can you tell if a player's active before the ball's kicked?'

And just like that I'm part of the group. I wonder if they're being nice (or Karl is) because I'm now a sad university dropout, but it seems more likely that they don't know or care about that. I offer to get in the next round, but they prefer to buy their own and not keep track of who's turn it is. So they're not trying to touch me for money, either.

I should stop being so suspicious and just accept them, like they seem to accept me.

I'm in the garage checking everything is set up right when I hear voices outside, a boy and a girl. I'm so relieved that I head straight for the door. It's not Gemma. It's a complete stranger who's walking beside Nathan. I'd forgotten that today was the day Erin was coming to meet us all.

'Hi,' I say, looking back at the road. 'Gemma not with you?'

'She said she had to walk that kid home.'

'Oh. Okay. Come in then.' I probably don't sound very welcoming but I'm sure now that Gemma won't turn up at all.

Erin has brought her bass guitar with her, which is good. I have one from when I was trying to lay down backing tracks for myself, but it's old and probably not in tune. She's a thin girl with dark, straight hair and glasses. She doesn't say much but when Nathan suggests we start with 'Ace Of Spades', because the bass in the intro is insane, Erin swings right into it. She goes from quiet nerd to frenzied guitarist in seconds.

'Brilliant,' I say when we finish a second run-through.

'Cool,' says Nathan, already looking sweaty.

'Jesus, do we have to play that song again?' Gemma is standing in the doorway, shaking out her umbrella.

I give her the biggest grin ever. 'We've done it twice already so you're excused for today.'

She says hi to the others and moves over to the keyboard, switching it on and checking the settings. She's only been using it a few weeks and she's already a pro.

'Let's try another cover,' I say. 'So Erin can get used to how we play. And then I'll try and do my song for you.'

'Sounds good,' says Nathan.

There are two advantages to having Erin playing with us. We definitely sound better with a bass, and she also seems to put Gemma at ease. Even though Gemma said she didn't know her well, just having another girl around changes the atmosphere. They can raise their eyebrows at each other when Nathan or I say something against Taylor Swift or Dua Lipa, and they can gang up on us when we want to try more heavy metal covers.

For the first time, we all go across to the house and have a coffee afterwards, so we can try to come up with a name for ourselves.

The three of them look around Mum's fancy kitchen, wide-eyed.

'Have a seat.' I indicate the tall, skinny stools at the breakfast bar. 'But make sure you don't fall off.'

Gemma climbs a stool as far away from me as possible. She keeps glancing towards the door to the hall.

'Both my parents are out,' I say.

She relaxes slightly and reaches for one of the ginger thins from the tin I've put out.

'Okay, a name,' I say. 'We want something new and different.' All suggestions so far have been completely ridiculous.

'I still think The Wankers would get attention,' says Nathan, snickering.

'Does this mean I'm in the band?' asks Erin, ignoring him.

'Yeah, if you want to be.'

Nathan is still rolling. 'Bandits, Vampires, Biscuits, The Cells, er ...'

'They don't feel right,' says Gemma.

Nathan looks sulky. 'So, what have you come up with? It's hard to think of a name for us when we're all so different.'

'The Mismatched?' says Gemma, and actually bursts out laughing. I love to hear her laugh.

'That's not bad,' says Erin.

'I'll put it on the list,' I say. Which means we've got precisely one possibility.

'It needs to be something that relates to us,' says Nathan.

'Two Gingers and a Swot,' says Erin, then glances at me. 'Sorry, that leaves you out.'

'Two Gingers, One Swot and The Head Boy,' says Nathan. He doesn't seem to mind the ginger label.

'Too long,' is all Gemma says.

'And I'm no longer head boy.'

'You're head boy of the band,' says Nathan. 'Hey, how about Head Boy and the somethings?'

'How about we leave this for now and concentrate on a set list.' Gemma seems completely at ease now.

I want it to stay that way, so I say, 'Okay, we need at least six songs if we're going to try and get a gig. And then we need to actually get a gig.'

'I think it's a bit early for that,' says Gemma. 'We need to do a lot more practising.'

'So how about we start meeting up twice a week?'

'You do remember Erin and Nathan and I have exams coming up?'

'Okay, one practice for now. And it'll probably take ages to find a gig so we need to start looking.'

Nathan says, 'How do you even start looking?'

We're quiet while we think about that.

'I remember there was an event in Kirkdouglas Town Hall,' says Gemma eventually. 'That guy Mark who plays bagpipes, his band were playing there.'

'Okay, I can ask him how that was arranged.'

'Some pubs do band sessions,' I say.

'Lily was talking about having a band night at the school,' says Nathan. 'To raise funds for something.'

'I can't play in front of the school,' yelps Gemma.

'What's the difference?' says Erin. 'Wherever we play round here it'll be mostly the same people.'

'I'm not sure ...'

I'm not having her back out now. 'The keyboard's always at the side of the stage. People will hardly see you.'

'But we can arrange to have some lighting on you—OW!' Nathan rubs his shin and glares at me. 'Did you just kick me?'

Erin looks from us to Gemma and back. She smiles. She must know what a brilliant musician Gemma is. And how shy.

'I think this is going to be fun,' she says. 'But now I have to go. Advanced Physics homework calls.'

Nathan stands up and Gemma says, 'I should go too.' She's definitely not going to stick around and talk to me. I don't make a big thing of it. I can be patient.

Gemma

I've been watching Rosie at school all week. Not in an obvious way, I hope, but just keeping an eye on her. I wasn't the only one. I could see Miss Reynolds, her class teacher, was concerned.

I don't see any of the other kids being nasty to her, but they don't include her either. When they chat in the classroom or run around in the playground, she's always on her own. On Thursday one of the older boys playing football runs right into her and knocks her to the ground. She grazes her knee and hand and has to come inside to be tended to. I don't think the boy did it on purpose. The other kids take no notice at all. It's like she's invisible.

'How's primary going?' asks Sarah when I go round on Thursday afternoon. 'Are you loving it to bits and have decided teaching is the career for you?'

'Rosie's really not happy.'

'Still? I thought she'd be better if she'd agreed to go back.'

'So did I.'

'What do you think is wrong?'

'I don't know. The other kids just kind of ignore her.'

Sarah frowns. 'If they're not bullying her, I suppose that's something.'

'But it's like it's a struggle for Rosie, every day, to go into the school. She watches the other kids playing and I'm sure she wants to join in but it's like she doesn't know how.'

Kids just *play*, don't they? They don't need instructions how to do it.

I sigh. 'I'm going to do some more research.'

'Google isn't the answer to everything, you know.'

'But it might be the answer to some things. Oh, and guess what, I've been learning about the rise in vegetarians and vegans. Did you know animal agriculture may be the number one cause of global warming? Not to mention factory farming is barbaric.'

Sarah raises her eyebrow. 'So you're serious about going veggie, then? I get why you'd want to, but I can't imagine making the change myself. Meat is too *good*.'

I continue to extol the virtues of going vegetarian for a while, even if I'm not totally sure I'll be able to stick to it myself. Really, there are so many things I'm not sure about. Including Rosie.

As I talk, I make a decision. I know how hard it can be to make connections with people when you're shy, especially people you don't know. I want to try and help Rosie. It seems like she struggles even more than I did.

On Friday I walk Rosie home from school and Mrs Thomson offers me a drink. I accept. I wonder if I dare ask her some questions? I'm not sure how to start but I'm hoping something will occur to me while I sip my orange juice.

'Can I go watch cartoons?' says Rosie in her soft voice. She'd answered her mum's questions about school with monosyllables.

Her mum sighs and says yes. This is my chance, especially when Mrs Thomson asks, 'How is she really? You've seen her in class as well as outside.'

I have to fight all my natural instincts to say everything is fine. 'She doesn't join in much.'

Mrs Thomson sighs again and shifts her mug around the table. 'She never does. She never has, really, but it seems worse since we moved here.'

I say cautiously, 'She seems like she wants to join in but doesn't know how.'

'I know.'

'I was wondering whether, well, if you thought maybe ...'

'What?'

'You've probably already thought of it. But ... has Rosie seen a doctor?' I grasp my hands together. I really don't want to offend her.

Mrs Thomson frowns. 'Like a psychologist? But

she's just shy.'

I want to say that she's not "just" shy, but I don't quite know how. She's struggling more than I ever I did, which is saying something. Before Lily befriended me, school was excruciating. Honestly, I could probably have done with help, and I think Rosie needs it now. But if her mum doesn't see it there's not much I can do.

I finish the last of my drink. 'Let me know if you want me to meet Rosie from school any time. And I'll see her for her lesson on Monday.'

'Thanks, Gemma.' She doesn't bother getting up to see me to the door.

Jamie

I've asked quite a few girls out. I've even been asked out by one or two. But I'm not sure I have the courage to ask Gemma out. What if she says no and it screws everything up? I can't work out if Gemma likes me and shyness is keeping her away. Or whether she genuinely does just want to be friends.

I go through various scenarios in my mind: Invite Gemma to see a movie. Invite her to go out for a drive. Go for a meal. It all feels too staged and serious, which is guaranteed to put her off. I want us to do something together, just the two of us, preferably away from Newton St Cuthbert. But I don't want to make a big thing of it because then I'm pretty sure she'll say no.

I manage to get her to walk the dogs with me, which is something. Except we can't go far because of Toby, and just when I'm trying to turn the conversation to us, the old dog goes sniffing between two massive rocks and doesn't seem to be able to back out.

'Oh god, Toby, no! Don't go there.' Gemma rushes forwards and tries unsuccessfully to lift him out. 'Now you're stuck! Sorry,' she says to me, like it's her fault. 'He's not very good at reversing.'

'Let me help.'

'No, he's muddy and disgusting.'

'So? He's also heavy. I can lift him.'

'If you're sure …'

We swap places and I manage to lift the idiot dog out, for which I get a growl.

'Thanks. So sorry about that. No, Toby, don't go down there!' The dog is now tottering towards a slope that drops steeply towards a stream.

'Maybe he wants a drink?'

'No, he doesn't.' Gemma is hanging on to him like she fears for his life. 'And I don't like long drops. Or water. Come on Toby. You don't really want to go down there.'

It seems she's right. Once she's turned the dog so he can see the path, he seems to forget all about the stream. I don't, though. I'm still thinking about what Gemma said, and remembering how she does seem to hang well back whenever we walk by the broad river that runs into the sea. 'It's only a shallow stream,' I point out. Gemma just shrugs. 'Maybe if you came sailing with me sometime, you'd see that water can be fun.'

'No.'

'Or we could go to the Galloway pool–'

'No! Look, I just don't like water, okay?'

It still seems weird to me, but I can see that even talking about it has upset her. 'Okay. I'm sorry.' I put my hand on her arm, hoping to offer comfort.

We walk in silence for a bit and I watch her biting her lip out of the corner of my eye. Finally, she sighs. 'Look, when I was little I was staying with my gran in Carlisle. The river near her house flooded. I was playing, I wasn't paying attention. And I slipped and fell in … I thought I was going to get washed away. I know it's silly and I should get over it but …'

I pull her close. 'It's not silly. Jesus, that must have been scary.'

'It's fine, it's not a problem. I just don't like water. Okay?' She takes a calming breath and moves away from me. 'Look, I'd better go back. Toby's really not up to long walks. Or walks of any kind, actually.'

Lucy is running way ahead so there's no chance of me cutting short my own walk.

When I do get home Mum's sitting in the kitchen, drinking black coffee and making lists.

'Jamie, I think it's time we had a talk.'

'Why?'

'Sit down, darling.'

'I need to …' *What can I say that will get her off my back?* 'Check my emails.' Which of course I really don't.

'This won't take long.' She pushes out one of the oak chairs with their fancy matching cushions.

I give in, as usual, and sit.

'I'm worried that you don't really seem to be thinking about your future. You've been home a couple of months now and I don't see you making any decisions. I know it's too late to apply for a uni place anywhere for the coming autumn, but you need to at least start thinking about what you want to do when you go back. Then you can tailor what you're doing with your time until then. That's what a gap year's for, you know. To gain experience that will help with your studies.'

'I thought it was about having fun.' It's funny how she now calls it a gap year, like it was all planned. 'And who says I want to go back to uni?'

She ignores that last bit completely. 'I'm talking about a *useful* gap year.'

'I'm working at the surgery, that's useful.'

'Part-time. I thought it might help you to see if there's anything in the medical field that interests you, but you don't seem that keen.'

'Mum, I'm doing filing in a back office! It has nothing to do with medicine. Which, by the way, I didn't want to do even if I *had* got the grades.'

'But there are associated careers. Paramedic. Physio. OT. Also nurses have far more opportunities open to them than in my day.'

'So why don't you go back to nursing?' There's a really bossy woman who works as a nurse practitioner at Dad's practice. I can definitely see Mum in that role.

'I've left it too long to go back. Whereas you have

209

your future before you. I just want to see you doing something with it.'

'I've set the band up,' I say. 'We're hoping to get some gigs soon.'

'Oh, the band,' she says. 'Good to get that out of your system, I suppose.'

I grit my teeth. 'And I'm reffing two or three matches a week.'

'But you're not getting the chance to do any big games down here, are you, like you were in Glasgow?'

I remember the fiasco of the one uni game I did. 'Maybe that's not the way I want to go with football. I enjoy a bit of reffing but there are other things. Gemma mentioned the primary school are on the lookout for someone to coach football to the kids.'

'Who's Gemma?'

'Friend of Lily's. She's in the band.'

'Lily's such a nice girl. It's a shame she and you broke up.'

It's not a shame at all, but I'm not going to get into that now. I stand up. 'Those emails won't check themselves.'

'You know, it wouldn't look bad on your CV, if you were to do coaching – voluntary work with school kids.'

'Mum, not everything is about what looks good on your CV.'

'Obviously, dear. But you do need to keep these things in mind.'

I roll my eyes. 'Anyway, it was just an idea.'

'It's a good one. Liz McQuarrie, the head teacher, comes to my book group. I'll have a chat with her.'

There it is again. The feeling that any ability to make my own decisions has been taken right away from me. Like the air has gone out of my lungs and the strength from my muscles.

I snap, 'Do not speak to Liz McQuarrie!'

'I'm only trying—'

'I haven't made up my mind yet. And when I do, I'll make any enquiries, not you. Okay?'

'If that's what you want, dear,' she says, looking hurt.

I know she means well, but I need to find a way of getting her off my case.

As I head upstairs, I think about Gemma. She avoids some things, but she pushes herself in other ways, like helping that kid Rosie.

I have this weird thought that I haven't ever pushed myself to help other people.

Maybe it's time to try.

Jamie

A couple of days later Mum actually comes up with something helpful. I'm making a sandwich after finishing my shift at the surgery when she says, 'I don't suppose you want to go and see *An Inspector Calls*?'

'What?'

'The play. Dad and I have tickets for the theatre in Kirkdouglas, but now he's got to go to Edinburgh and I thought I'd go with him. Make a weekend of it. You'll be all right here on your own, won't you?'

'I'll be fine,' I say immediately. A weekend on my own? Bring it on! And then I remember her original question. 'So when's this theatre thing?'

'Friday evening.'

'And you've got two tickets?'

'That's right. Do you want to go? You could ask Lily if she wanted to go along? She's very interested in drama, isn't she?'

'A few of that crowd are. I'll find someone to go with.'

Amazingly, she's too caught up in her weekend away in the capital to ask any further questions. She'll get to see Michael while she's up there, so he can put up with her.

Now I just need to persuade Gemma she wants to spend an evening watching a play I've never even heard of. And as Friday is tomorrow, I can't waste any time.

Jamie: You doing anything tomorrow night? Mum's given me two tickets for the theatre in Kirkdouglas.

She doesn't answer immediately. She's probably trying to think of a suitable excuse. I can see that she's read the message.

Eventually she replies.

Gemma: Is it An Inspector Calls? A few of us were planning to go on Saturday. Donny has a part in it.

Jamie: That's the one. Come with me on Friday. You'll be doing me a favour. I don't want to go on my own.

Another long pause where I really really want to know what she's thinking. Then:

Gemma: OK, if you want. I'll tell Lily to give my Saturday ticket to someone else.

I make arrangements to pick Gemma up the following evening, and then send her links to a couple of songs I've been thinking we could cover. I want to keep the chat going, even if it is interrupting her studying or whatever it is she does in an evening.

I never used to wonder what Gemma Anderson did with her evenings.

At least I know that tomorrow she'll be spending it with me.

Gemma

Mum is the only person I tell who I'm going to the play with, and she just raises her eyebrows. That's one of the many good things about Mum. She's cheery and chatty but she doesn't interfere in my life unless she thinks I'm going to do something really stupid. Which going out for the evening with Jamie hopefully isn't.

I keep trying to tell myself that it's just an evening out as friends. Using up some tickets his mum had. That's not a date, is it?

But when I stand in my room, staring into my wardrobe, it *feels* like a date. And it's impossible to decide on an outfit. Nothing feels right: too smart, too casual, too clingy, wrong colour. Why did I ever think I could wear bright colours with hair like mine? But Lily used to say I wear too much black and grey, and I have to agree with her.

I've now got fifteen minutes before Jamie is due to pick me up (which also makes this seem like a date) and

I'm in a complete tizz. My phone buzzes and I actually hope it's him, calling it off. In half an hour I might be disappointed, but right now it would just be a relief.

It's Sarah.

Sarah: Want to come over and watch a trashy movie?

Obviously the answer is no, and I'm hardly even worried about telling her why. I need help, fast. I call her.

'Can you come over here?'

'To watch a movie?'

'No. I need you to tell me what to wear.'

I just need a second opinion. And Sarah won't cross-question me like Lily would.

'Wear for what?'

Or maybe she will.

'For the theatre in Kirkdouglas.'

'Tomorrow? Why the hurry?'

I say reluctantly, 'Actually, I'm going tonight.'

'Oh.' Tiny pause. 'Who with?'

There's no help for it. 'Jamie Abernethy.'

'Oh my god! Go you! So you *are* getting friendly with him.'

'A bit. Because of the band. His mum had some tickets. It's nothing.'

'Ri-iiight.' She leaves me hanging with her doubt loud and clear. Then she laughs. 'I'll be right over!'

'Be quick. He's picking me up in ten minutes.'

She must have started walking while we were speaking, because thirty seconds later she's in my bedroom. 'Show me what you've got.'

I do as I'm told. It's one of my skills, honed over years of friendship with Lily. Plus if you can't make a decision for yourself then you have to go with the advice you've asked for.

I'm fairly happy with the result. Sarah suggests black jeans and ankle boots, then a green velvety wrap-around top that I would never have dared to wear but looks okay.

Sarah stands back to admire her work and says, 'No hiding away in that big cardi that absolutely drowns you, okay? You look great.'

I don't have time to argue, even though I would have loved to throw my knee-length baggy favourite over everything. I even put on mascara, because she insists. Good thing I invested in a nice new one.

'Are you sure?' I say as I hear the car pull up outside.

'You'll be fine,' she says firmly. 'Have fun.' Then she pushes me out of the door before I have time to ask her not to say anything to Lily. Although I'm not sure I would have asked anyway. That would just be making this out to be a big thing, when it's not.

Jamie is wearing double denim and a scarf that muffles his face. I immediately feel overdressed. If he's just wearing a T-shirt under that jacket, I'll know I am.

'Ever seen this play before?' he asks cheerfully.

'No.'

'Me neither. I hope it's not all worthy and serious.

Be just typical of Mum if it was.'

'Donny said something about it being "a biting social satire".'

'What does that even mean?'

We glance at each other and suddenly we're laughing. 'I have absolutely no idea,' I admit. 'Still, it'll be fun to watch Donny, even if the rest of the play is crap.'

'He must be good if he got into the Conservatoire.'

'He is. Acting's about the only thing he takes seriously. At least someone knows what they want to do with their life.' I tell myself not to think about that now. I'm spending the evening with Jamie. And if anyone can help me enjoy myself and take my mind off the future for a while, it's him.

Jamie

'We don't have to stay till the end,' I say during the interval. This place is way overheated and I've already had to roll up the sleeves of my shirt.

'We can't leave! I think Donny's big performance comes in the final act.'

'Bit grim though, isn't it? Not a bunch of laughs.'

'That's because it's meant to be ... *biting social satire!*' I join Gemma on that last bit, grinning.

I continue. 'But it's all a bit last century, isn't it? People aren't such snobs nowadays.' When she doesn't answer I stoop to see her expression more clearly. 'What? Are they?'

'Well, it's probably not as bad as it was then. But there are still class differences, aren't there? Look at you and Lily with your posh parents and big houses.'

'I'm not posh!'

She shrugs. 'Your dad's a doctor.'

'My parents are no better off than Lily's, in fact

probably not as well off. And you're friends with her so you can't hold it against me.'

'I'm not holding it against you,' she says quickly.

Much as I'd like to laugh at the idea of myself as some kind of landed gentry, I really hope this isn't going to be one more reason for Gemma to think that she and I don't go together.

The bell rings for the interval to end so we have to go back and sit down before I can nip that in the bud.

The best thing I can say about the play is that Donny Miller is bloody brilliant. The whole cast are amateurs, and with most of them you can tell. Not Donny. He's no longer in-your-face, floppy-haired and camp. He's an arrogant, wealthy young drunkard, who gradually accepts responsibility for the death of a woman. His English accent, his mannerisms, his gradual evolution – they're amazing.

Afterwards Gemma and I hurry out of the foyer, mainly because I want to avoid any of my parents' friends who might want to make intelligent conversation about the play.

'Donny was great,' Gemma says. 'I don't think I realised quite how good he is. I've only ever seen him in school stuff, mostly comedies.'

'Aye, he was good. I don't suppose you're eighteen yet, are you?'

She squints up at me, thrown by the sudden change of topic. 'No. Not till next month. Why?'

'I just thought we could go for a drink somewhere.

D'you think you could pass for eighteen? Are there any pubs that don't ID much?'

She shakes her head. 'Even when I am eighteen, I won't pass for it.'

She's probably right. Tonight she's wearing the faintest touch of make-up and and high heels, but you wouldn't put her above sixteen.

Because she seems disheartened, I say, 'You'll probably be one of those people that looks young all their lives.'

'I'll probably be one of those gingers whose hair goes grey when they're thirty.'

I touch her hair, which she has pinned up. 'Not ginger. Strawberry blonde? Burnished copper?'

'Oooh, look at you, all arty.' She bats my hand away but I see her blush slightly.

She feels our connection, I'm sure she does. I don't want the evening to end yet.

'There's that hotel on the edge of town. We can go there for a coffee and cake or something.'

'I don't want to have coffee so late.'

'Something else then? Come on, why not?'

I take her hand. She doesn't object.

Gemma

This is turning more and more into a date, and that's making me nervous. And scared. And happy. But mostly nervous.

We said we were just going to be friends and I could cope with that. Anything more is frankly terrifying. The problem isn't his posh parents and big house, although they don't help. It's the fact that he's Jamie – best looking boy in his year; popular, outgoing, sporty … Everything I'm not.

He can't possibly want to be with me.

So why is he spending time with me?

'You're quiet,' he says, when we've been given a table in the restaurant. I would *never* have dared come somewhere like this just for dessert. The waiter didn't even bat an eye when Jamie asked for the dessert menu. I don't know if that's because he's Jamie or because doing that is actually okay.

I look around the room, at the white tablecloths

and sparkling glass and silverware. It's no longer very busy, but there are still a handful of people, all grown-ups.

'I'd never have thought to come here.'

'Is it okay? Don't you like it?'

'It's lovely,' I say quickly. I don't want him to think I don't appreciate the effort.

The waiter comes to take our order. I have tiramisu and camomile tea, Jamie has apple pie and black coffee. His choice relaxes me a bit. Apple pie is normal. I can make apple pie. Maybe I could make apple pie for him some time.

'I wonder how easy it is to make tiramisu,' I say, as I take a tiny first mouthful. Delicious. Creamy and bitter at the same time.

'No idea.'

'I could try it. I don't think there can be many ingredients. Coffee – ha! So I am having coffee – and sponge and, I don't know, crème fraiche? Ricotta?'

'You seem to know a lot about food.'

'Not really, but I like cooking. Well, baking. Here, try some, this is really good.' I push my plate towards him, not really thinking, just wanting him to share in the pleasure.

He takes a spoonful and tries it, closing his eyes. 'Wow. That is good.'

I'm watching him so that when he opens his eyes again he's looking straight into mine. It all feels too intimate. I blush.

He smiles and pushes his plate towards me. 'Try some of this? It's not as special as yours, but it's okay.'

I'm thankful to have something to distract me, even if it does mean leaning towards him, taking food off his plate with my fork. I desperately don't want him to realise how my stomach is doing little excited flips because he's so near.

'How's the reffing going?' I say. There. Nothing remotely flirtatious about that.

He sits back in his seat, still watching me with that heart-stopping smile. 'It's fine, I'm getting regular matches. There's a possibility of me being an assistant ref for a senior match in Annan.'

'That's great. I'm sure you'd be amazing.'

He shrugs. 'We'll see. Hey, you know you said they needed someone to coach football at the primary school? Do you know if they've found anyone?'

'I don't know. I doubt it.'

'I was wondering about offering to help out.'

'That would be wonderful.' Jamie is just the kind of person those kids need to get them organised, encourage them.

'I'm not a proper coach or anything, but I probably know enough to help kids.'

'I'm sure they'd be delighted. You should speak to Mrs McQuarrie, the head teacher. Do you know her?'

'No, but Mum does.' He grimaces. 'Do you have her contact details? It'd be good to get in there and arrange things myself, before Mum starts taking over.'

'I'm sure she's only trying to help.'

He shrugs. 'Anyway, never mind that. Got any more ideas for band names?'

'I still think we should go for Mismatched.'

'I quite liked Map Fighters.' Erin had found a band name generator site that came up with some really appalling names. Map Fighters was one of the better ones.

'It's got nothing to do with us. We don't read maps, we don't fight.'

'Band names aren't mean to be taken literally, you know. Although I quite liked Vegan Guitars.'

'None of us are vegan.'

'*Yet*. Isn't the whole world turning vegan?'

'I don't know.' I scrape up the last tiny morsel of my dessert. I'm glad I'm not vegan right now.

'Aside from the name, we need to agree a list of songs to cover,' says Jamie. 'People need to be familiar with at least some of the stuff we choose.'

'We could do some older stuff, maybe a Beatles cover. Everyone knows the Beatles.' He and Nathan are far too keen on those weird shouty songs.

'I thought you'd be more into Bach than the Beatles.' Jamie says playfully.

'Nah. Has to be Rabbie Burns or the Beatles. I did a really cool orchestration of 'Yesterday' for my National 5.'

'Only someone completely weird would put Burns and the Beatles in the same sentence.' He grins at me, like being weird is a good thing. Even though this conversation is absurd, I'm enjoying it. I'm daring to be myself and not worrying that I'll have nothing to say.

On the drive back to Newton St Cuthbert we're still bickering about band names and songs. I want to put on some Jellyman's Daughter for him to listen to and he wants me to branch out and try Hurts. Even the name puts me off.

It's only when he pulls up in front of my house that reality intrudes. It's dark, and most houses have their curtains drawn, but I immediately feel like there's a spotlight on me, that everyone is peering out. Sarah in particular.

'Thanks. That was great.' I fumble for the door latch. I need to get out before …

'I enjoyed it too. Thanks for coming.' Jamie sounds … polite? Distant? At the very least *not* like he's about to pounce on me, which makes my nervousness feel ridiculous. Nevertheless, I jump out the second I manage to get the car door open.

'Thanks again!' I shout. 'Bye!'

I think he says goodbye, too, but I've already let the door close and am heading up our short path. I turn when I get to the front door and raise a hand. Only then does he drive away. And now I wish I'd thanked him properly, maybe even invited him in for a drink. Ha! As if I'd ever have the courage to do that.

Everybody seems to have gone to bed so I let Toby out for a last widdle and then take myself upstairs. It feels like an anti-climax. I'd dreaded the evening, but then it was so much fun. Now it's over, with no plans to do it again.

I wonder why he didn't even try to kiss me?

Gemma

I don't sleep well and head downstairs late the following morning.

'How was the play?' says Mum, who seems to be doing a spring clean of the kitchen.

'Good, really good. Donny was amazing.' I realise I should have messaged him to say so. I've been way too self- (or Jamie-) obsessed.

I take the tea and toast back up to my room and message Donny with over-the-top praise, hoping that will make up for the lateness of it. I want to message Jamie too, to thank him for the evening. But I already thanked him in person and I didn't want to overdo it, or make it seem like I've spent this morning thinking about last night. I need some other reason for contacting him. We have band practice tomorrow, but that doesn't feel soon enough.

Speaking of which, Lily has been talking again about a possible band night at school. I could approach her about our band being in it. But the few half-conversations I've had with Lily recently have not gone well. If I make the effort to contact her now, is she going to think that I'm admitting I've been in the wrong?

I sigh. How can something as straightforward as my friendship with Lily have got so complicated?

I message her to see if she's free. She is. Okay, it looks like I'm going to do this. I head into town, growing more nervous the nearer I get to her house.

Lily opens the door and just stands there. 'Hey. You came.' She must have known I would. I get the feeling she just doesn't know what else to say, which is very unlike her. As is the way she's smiling at me, all unsure. Her head is on one side like she's trying to work me out. 'It's good to see you,' she says.

She gestures for me to enter and leads the way to the kitchen. 'Tea? Juice?' Her mum is there, looking as elegant and dreamy as always.

'Afternoon Gemma,' she says.

'Afternoon.'

'Mum and I have been in Dumfries this morning,' says Lily. 'For a dance lesson. Can you believe it? Me, dancing. I remembered most of the steps this time, didn't I, Mum?'

'And you were almost in time with the music,' says her mother, smiling her beautiful smile.

'Are you enjoying it?' I'm suddenly put out that

things have been happening in Lily's life that I don't know about.

Mrs Hildebrand says, 'It was hard to begin with, but I am enjoying it now.'

'That's because you're a natural,' says Lily grumpily. 'Why can't I take after you rather than Dad?'

'Your dad is actually not a bad dancer. And you just need more practice.'

Lily doesn't look convinced, but Mrs Hildebrand smiles and says she'll leave us in peace. Once the kitchen door has closed behind her, an awkward silence falls.

I open my mouth to say something – anything – but Lily takes a deep breath and blurts out, 'Listen, before you ask whatever it is you've come for, I want to say something.'

'Yes?' I squeeze my hands together. What if she starts making suggestions or telling me I'm the reason things have gone between us?

'I'm sorry,' she says.

I stare at her. 'What?'

'You don't need to sound so surprised!' She gives a faint smile, sounding a bit more like herself. 'I am capable of apologising you know.'

'What are you apologising for exactly?' Part of me wants to accept the apology with no questions asked. The other part wants her to acknowledge why she owed me one in the first place.

'I'm sorry I went on at you about the Conservatoire

and everything. Tom kept telling me that it was your decision and to leave it alone, but I honestly thought that you were making a massive mistake and that I was being helpful.'

'And now?'

'Well I wasn't being helpful, was I?'

'No, I mean do you still think I made a mistake?'

'I ...' She trails off, opening her mouth several times without actually continuing her answer. Finally, looking reluctant, she says, 'Maybe? I don't really know. But I guess that's the point, isn't it? I *don't* know what's right for you. I just know that my dream was the Conservatoire, so I couldn't understand why it wasn't yours when you'd got in and I hadn't.'

I'm grinning. I don't care that she isn't rushing to tell me I made the right choice – I don't need her to. I care that she's finally going to accept my choice either way. 'I still think they were mad not to take you,' I tell her.

'Thanks. But I'm okay about it now. I think Politics or Media might be more my kind of thing, you know?'

'Politics,' I say instantly. 'You should do Politics.'

'And you should stop telling me what to do!' Lily says with mock anger.

We're both grinning like two lunatics now. I move to hug her. Thank goodness. Oh, thank goodness. She hugs me back hard. I can feel a lump in my throat.

When she pulls away she's still smiling. 'Right. So now why don't you tell me what it was you came round here for?'

'I came to ask you a favour.'

'Ask away.' She sits down on one of the kitchen chairs, her leg swinging, her eyes bright.

'It's about the band night at school. Are we having one?'

'Maybe. Why?'

'Jamie's band, I mean our band, is looking for somewhere to perform.'

She raises an eyebrow. '*Your* band, is it? Interesting. We've identified two potential Fridays in May. Mr Barrett's fine with us using the school hall. The problem is no one wants to take on the organising and I'm busy with the prom committee and head girl stuff.'

'And exams.'

'And those. Plus I want to screen a movie in the hall to see whether people would be interested in running it as a regular thing.'

I laugh. 'You don't have time!'

She pulls a face and laughs too. 'I know I don't. That's why I'm getting nowhere with the band night idea. You know, you could take it on. You'd be able to select the bands and decide on the running order – you'd have complete control. What do you think?'

It would be masses of work, but I'm tempted. This would mean we have a gig. 'Would I have to have a committee?'

'Up to you.'

'I'll do it if I don't have to have a committee. And if I can talk things over with you when I'm not sure of anything.'

'I thought you didn't like talking things over with me.' She's still smiling, but there's an honest question there too.

I clear my throat. 'Just don't try to push me to do things I don't want to and we'll be fine.'

'Deal.' She sticks out her hand and we actually shake on it. 'Right. I could take the earlier Friday for my film night, and the band night can be the last Friday in May, which should be okay for exam people. Band night will be mostly older kids, whereas film night could be for anyone. Sound good?'

I get my phone out so that I can check the dates. Lily takes some cans out of the fridge and we head out into the garden so we can plan some more. It's lovely to be sitting with Lily in her garden again.

When I finally get up to go, Lily says, 'I hope Jamie appreciates what you're doing.'

'I'm not just doing it for Jamie.'

'Well the band, then. And you know, Gem, I wouldn't mind if you and Jamie were getting … *friendly*. I don't care that he's my ex or any of that stuff. I just don't want you to get hurt.'

'There's nothing to get hurt about.'

She narrows her eyes, like she can laser through my words to my thoughts. Thank goodness she can't.

Eventually all she says is, 'So I can confirm the band night with Mr Barrett on Monday?'

'Go for it.'

Jamie

It was only when I got home from the play that I realised I hadn't made any plans to see Gemma again. Which means I'm wasting a really good opportunity, because I have the house to myself all weekend. I think about messaging her on Saturday morning, but I don't want to come on too pushy.

I take Lucy for a run and then go over to the music room to try out a new song. I've got the first line in my head, *How do I know what you're thinking?* Or maybe that'll be the chorus. It's going to be kind of plaintive but catchy, if I can just get the right beat behind it.

It's literally hours later when I come to. I've been so absorbed in the music I haven't thought about anything else, haven't heard a thing. But something must have distracted me …

There's a knock on the side door, for what must be at least the second time.

'Come in,' I shout, putting aside my guitar.

The door opens slowly, hesitantly, to reveal Gemma.

I jump to my feet. 'Hi! Hello!' I'm so pleased to see her that I want to rush over and catch her in my arms, but even these two words of greeting send her back a step.

'Er, hi. Sorry to disturb you.'

'You're not disturbing me. I'm working on a new song. Come in and listen.' I go and sit back down, to show that I'm not going to leap on her, and she enters the room properly.

'I wasn't sure there was anyone home. And then I heard you playing.'

'The parents are away so it's just me. Come and tell me what you think of this. It's still very rough.'

She perches on the edge of the armchair and I start playing. I have a moment of doubt because this song is about Gemma, and I really don't want her to know that. I fumble my way through it, playing the verse and the chorus and then the chorus again, because that's as far as I've got.

When I finish there's silence. I say quickly, 'Like I said, it's only rough, and that's the acoustic version, so ...'

'It's really good!' Her eyes are shining. Even if she doesn't know it's about her, she likes it. 'I don't know how you do it. I can play other people's music, but I just can't seem to write my own.'

'It was just an idea I had.' I'm pleased and embarrassed by her praise. I put the guitar aside. 'I need to check up on Lucy. I didn't realise how long I've been out here. Come over to the house.'

The house seems very quiet and private with just the two of us. I let Lucy out into the back garden and head to the fridge. 'Orange juice? Irn-Bru? Beer?'

'Juice would be good.'

I get the drinks and we sit side by side at the table. There's a silence that feels awkward, like neither of us knows what to say next. I get up to let Lucy back in and Gemma starts flicking through a magazine Mum has left there.

'Ow! Ow, shit.' She jumps and frowns down at her hand.

'What is it?'

'Nothing. Just a paper cut.'

I can see blood welling along the thin cut on her finger. She holds it out like it's a great injury, feeling for a tissue with her other hand. Which, being Gemma, she finds. She dabs the wound. 'Who would have thought a paper cut would cause so much blood?'

I can't help saying, 'It's not that much blood.'

'I hate the sight of blood.' She dabs it again, even though it's already stopped bleeding. Then she catches my expression and gives a weak smile. 'I'm being an idiot, aren't I? My brother says I'm a hypochondriac.'

I reach out and take the wounded hand and look at it. There's barely a scratch, but I get a plaster from Mum's first aid drawer and carefully apply it.

'Sorry,' Gemma mutters. 'I was being stupid.'

She hasn't pulled her hand away. She might be blushing slightly, but she's not retreating. I lean closer and kiss her cheek, and still she doesn't withdraw. I feel like she's holding her breath, nervous but not unwilling.

'Can I kiss you?' I whisper. I do not want a repeat of that time at Lily's party.

She meets my eyes, blushing fiery red, still not withdrawing. She leans in. 'Yes.'

And then we're really kissing. Beautiful Gemma is in my arms, her lips hungry against mine, and everything feels right.

After a while I make myself pull back. I'm feeling a bit breathless and Gemma looks quite wild, her eyes wide, her hair in a mess around her shoulders.

'Wow,' says Gemma.

'Yeah. Wow, hey?' I smile and kiss her again, just briefly.

'Can you stay long?' I ask. 'I don't want you to go yet.'

She blushes again. 'There's no rush.'

'Stay for the evening. We can watch a movie. My parents are away.' I shouldn't have reminded her of that, it might worry her.

She doesn't look worried though. She's looking about, smiling. 'What about food? Can we eat here?'

'Mum left stuff in the freezer for me to heat up.'

'I'll make something fresh,' she says. 'You've got eggs. I can make us an omelette. With a salad? Will it be okay for me to see what's in the fridge?'

'Sure.' I have absolutely no idea what's in the fridge barring things to drink.

She stands up and begins rooting around. She seems pleased with what she finds. 'Mushrooms. And parmesan. I can definitely make something with this. Is that okay?'

'It's more than okay.' I really like seeing this new, quietly confident Gemma. 'But first we need to take Lucy for a short walk. Oh, and you can tell me why you called round. Unless it was for this?' I loop my arms around her from behind and kiss her again.

'Of course not. Don't be ridiculous.' She blushes again.

'So tell me why you came to see me.'

She frowns, like she's almost forgotten. 'It was about the school band night. I got Lily to agree on a date for it, and we're definitely on the list. In fact, I'm sort of in charge of the whole thing, so we could be the lead act.'

I'm impressed. 'So we've got one definite gig lined up?'

'Seems like it. Unless you're not interested, in which case no problem, I'll canc–'

'Don't you dare!'

She giggles and jumps away as I try to tickle her.

Nothing's been said, no big declarations – that wouldn't feel right with Gemma, but everything's different now. I take her hand automatically as we walk Lucy. We laugh and kiss and tease, and I can feel myself grinning like an eejit.

Gemma Anderson likes me. Which is just as well because I *really* like her.

Gemma

I walk home on a cloud, so happy and amazed I want to sing out loud. There is a tiny corner of my mind saying *this can't be happening* and *this will all go wrong,* but it's so tiny and my heart feels so big that I can ignore it.

I'm so glad I didn't go to the play with Lily and the others tonight. I'm so glad I dropped by Jamie's on the way back from hers before I could talk myself out of it. And thank goodness his parents weren't there. We got to curl up on the settee uninterrupted, arms wrapped around each other. I've never kissed anyone properly before, never wanted to be so close. It felt amazing. Even the memory of his lips against mine sends tingles right through me.

I am not going to overthink this. This is good. The band night is going to be good. Things with Lily are good.

Life is good.

Jamie

Gemma comes around before band practice on Sunday so we have some time together. There's a bit of kissing and a lot of laughing as we play around with some new songs. When the others arrive, Gemma goes quiet. I follow her lead and don't touch her or look at her any more than normal, although I can't believe they don't realise something is different. Everything feels different to me.

The practice goes well. Unfortunately, Gemma can't stay after as she's doing something with that kid Rosie. I get her to give me the contact details for Mrs McQuarrie. If Gemma can take on organising band nights, I can definitely take on a bit of football coaching. I send an email offering to help out. What I don't expect is one back within ten minutes asking for my mobile number so she can phone me. Or that fifteen minutes after that I'll be signed up for my first coaching session on Tuesday afternoon! That woman certainly doesn't give you the chance to change your mind. It'll be a mixed group, and apparently Mrs McQuarrie herself has a daughter who's keen to play. Everyone is going to be so happy.

I message Gemma who replies with all the positive emojis.

Gemma: That's brilliant. Bet Mrs McQuarrie's delighted to have you.

Jamie: She's delighted to have anyone. She's really keen to get girls playing as well as boys. Might be helpful if you were there as my assistant coach.

Gemma: I know absolutely nothing about football!

Jamie: I'll give the instructions. All you'd have to do is be encouraging.

Gemma: I really don't think it's my kind of thing.

I play my trump card.

Jamie: You could bring Rosie along. Didn't you say she needed to get involved in more school stuff?

There's a long pause, which I take as a positive sign. Eventually she messages.

Gemma: I'll think about it and let you know. What time?

Yep, definitely a good sign.

I could tell Mum about the coaching, she'd be delighted, but I don't feel like facing her approval, which will undoubtedly be followed by her suggestions. Spring seems to have finally appeared, so I head down to the sailing club to see if there's a boat I can take out. There is, but as the commodore is doing me a favour by lending it to me, I have to reciprocate by helping the Sunday afternoon kids dismantle their boats first. I can see John watching me and nodding approvingly. It doesn't take a genius to know he's hoping I'll volunteer to do some sailing tuition sometime soon.

I take out one of the Mirror dinghies and tack out of the estuary, enjoying the sound of the wind in the sail and the smell of the sea. I wish Gemma was here. I should offer to teach her to sail again. I know why she's afraid of water now, but I haven't given up on helping her get over it.

Gemma

I coax Rosie into going along to Jamie's football coaching session on Tuesday. Unfortunately that means I have to go too, for support. I also have the bright idea of getting Sarah to come along too. She's still doing better, and she's sporty, which I'm definitely not.

At the end of school, I make my way reluctantly out of the back gate of the Academy. Apart from worrying about how to behave around Jamie (he wouldn't kiss me in public, would he?), I'm really not keen on having anything to do with football. What if I get hit by the ball?

By the time I reach the primary school playing fields, there are about twenty kids gathered in sports gear. Jamie is looking fit in a tracksuit, with piles of balls and bibs at his feet. Seeing him makes my heart give a little kick. One of the teachers I know is introducing him to the kids. Sarah is there already. She's carrying a massive stack of plastic cones and I can't help saying, 'Should you be doing that?' She's dressed in jeans and a hoody, but beneath all the layers you can see how skinny she still is.

'Why not? Don't you think I can?'

Oops, I need to remember not to say things like that. I was the one who encouraged her to come. I just don't want her to overdo things. I take half the cones for myself. 'Tell me where to put them.' I'm glad she's here. The teacher is now 'supervising' from the pavilion – in other words catching up on her marking. I'd feel far too self-conscious if it was just Jamie and me with all the kids.

Rosie is also there, standing apart as usual. She gives me a very slight smile and then looks down again. I call out a hello and gesture her forwards.

Jamie divides the youngsters into groups of three or four and gets them to spread out and pass the ball between them. Rosie, predictably, ends up without a group but Jamie's not having that. He inserts her into one with three other girls and makes them do passes in a certain pattern, so there's no way they can exclude her.

He comes over to Sarah and me. 'Great that you're both here. We'll be able to get the kids to do more if we can divide them between the three of us.'

'I'm just here to watch,' I say.

'Rubbish.' And he grins at me in that way that makes my heart skip. He's wearing his cap on backwards and looking extra cute, which doesn't help. 'I'm doing this exercise to get an idea of their ball skills, which are obviously variable. I'm going to set the better ones up to play a five-a-side game over there, and the rest will do more drills using the cones Sarah's put out.'

He's in his element. He doesn't mind telling the kids what to do, and as they're here voluntarily they're all keen enough to obey. Sarah and I are given separate groups to work with, getting the ball around the cones or passing and attempting to score. Some of the kids are completely useless but they're having a good time. I'm running up and down a fair bit myself. I wish I was in jeans and trainers like Sarah, and not my nice new shoes that I really don't want to get mud on.

I keep an eye on Rosie. She's definitely one of the least adept. She's tall and gangly and she misses the ball as often as she hits it. But her tongue's sticking out the side of her mouth like it does when she's concentrating at piano, so she is trying. On her second shot at goal, she scores. For a moment she just looks startled, then she gives a little jump of excitement. The boy in goals says, 'That was a fluke,' but the girl behind Rosie says, 'No it wasn't, you were in the wrong place.'

I'm pleased that she's standing up for Rosie, but Rosie has already moved away. She doesn't engage with any of the other children, even when they're talking directly to her. Most of the time they just ignore her, and I can't really blame them. If she's not going to try, why should they? They're only kids after all.

Apart from Rosie, the whole session goes pretty well. Sarah seems to be enjoying herself, the kids are learning something, and Jamie even gives them stuff to practise before the next session. He's an excellent teacher. I remember Lily saying that when he was helping the kids learn to sail last summer, he talked too much and didn't listen. I don't know if he's changed since then, or if Lily was just biased. Now he's joking with the kids and asking for ideas and checking who the school team have played against so far. The boys do most of the talking, flattered to have an older boy taking an interest, but Jamie makes sure the girls have a chance too.

Sarah says in a low voice, as we wait for him to dismiss them, 'He's not a bad coach.'

I smile because she's echoing my own thoughts. 'I know.'

'Not bad looking either.'

'I kno– Sarah!'

She laughs. 'You know what I'd like to do? I'd like to be one of those girls playing football. It looks so much fun, doesn't it?'

I don't think it looks fun at all, but I'm happy to be encouraging. 'Maybe you'll be able to start playing, soon.'

'But girls my age don't play, do they? It's okay at primary school, when boys and girls play together. It's not the same at high school.'

'Aren't there girls' football teams?' It's not something I've ever thought about.

'I've never heard of any in Newton St Cuthbert.'

'Then you should start one once you're back at school.' I seem to be channelling Lily in a very concerning way.

'Maybe. If I'm ever well enough.' She kicks the ground. She doesn't like me worrying about her, but she's still not that confident herself.

'Why shouldn't you be? You're feeling okay now, aren't you?'

'I'm fine. Although I'd better head home before Mum sends out a rescue party.'

I realise Rosie is standing halfway between the rest of the kids and Sarah and me. Even with all the effort to involve her, she's still doing nothing. I can't help but feel frustrated. Sarah has problems but at least she tries to do something about them.

As Sarah heads off, I shout across the field, 'Rosie, why don't you help collect the bibs?' Then when she just stands and looks at me dumbly, I wave my arms. 'Come on!'

One of the girls says, 'Yeah. Be nice if you did help for once.'

A couple of the others snigger. Rosie closes her eyes.

The girls lose interest and go back to their task. I know I felt annoyed with Rosie before for not making an effort, but now I'm cross with the girls. That wasn't kind.

'It's fine, Rosie,' I say encouragingly, trying to mend the damage I realise I've done with my impatience. 'Come with me to get the cones.'

She doesn't move. Her eyes are still tightly shut. I move towards her, worried that tears are starting, but before I get near, she's turned away. She starts walking, and then running, towards the gate. I try to catch up with her, calling out, but she's fast. Shit! As far as I know, she's never gone home on her own before. I shout to Jamie and head off after her.

I catch up with Sarah whose already on her way home. 'Did you see Rosie?'

'Yeah, she ran past. I think she was crying. Should I have stopped her?'

There's no sign of Rosie when I reach her house so I knock on the front door. After what seems like a unreasonably long time, Mrs Thomson answers.

'Did Rosie come home?' I ask, even though I can hear crying from inside.

'Yes. I thought you were going to walk her back?'

'I'm sorry. She just ran off.'

'Thanks for checking, Gemma. She says she doesn't want to see you.' And she closes the door.

Jamie

Coaching was fun. The kids were a laugh, and I felt like I was doing something useful. It's a shame Gemma left before I had the chance to talk to her, but I'll see her again soon.

When I get home, Mum is waiting for me. 'Where have you been? I expected you back ages ago.'

'I was coaching the primary school kids, I told you.'

'That is good of you, dear. But look at this. Mike Maynard, who has his own accountancy firm in Dumfries, is looking for a trainee to work with him. If you're serious about not going back to uni, this could be just the thing for you. It'd be full-time, and with a good job at the end of it.'

She pushes the advert towards me. I don't even glance at it.

'I've already phoned Mike. Your dad knows him from Rotary. He's willing to give you an interview. I thought tomorrow afternoon?'

She smiles at me, pleased with herself, sure I'll just fit in with her plans.

The anger rises up so quickly it almost chokes me. 'No.'

'What do you mean no? Really, Jamie, this is ideal.'

'No,' I say again. I take a breath. 'That isn't what I want to do.'

'You don't know what you want to do, do you? So why not—'

'I'm not going for the interview.'

'But I've already arranged it!'

'Then you can un-arrange it. And you can stop interfering in my life!' I'm shouting now. 'I'm eighteen, nearly nineteen, stop trying to run my life for me!'

'Please don't speak to me like that.'

'It's the only way I can get you to listen!' I spin around and leave the room. If I don't do that I might start throwing something. I bang the door on my way out, hard. Jesus, she knows how to destroy a good mood. I shut myself in my bedroom and put on some loud music.

Later there's a knock on the door. It can't be Mum, because she'd come straight in. I turn down the music, 'Yes?'

Dad comes in and closes the door. 'Jamie, your mother is very upset.'

'So?' I'd love to be able to match his calm and measured tone, but I can't. 'That makes two of us.'

'Do you want to talk about it?'

'No, I don't want to talk about it. Mum's a nightmare. I'm not a child to be told what to do every minute of the day.'

'Jamie, while you are living at home with us, you have to respect your mother's wishes. She is just trying to help.'

'Why do you have to take her side? Why don't you stand up to her and tell her to stop being an interfering cow?'

'Please don't speak about your mother like that.'

I find myself calming down a bit. That's the effect Dad has. 'How can she think I'd want that job? I'm not going to the interview.'

'You don't need to. Perhaps your mother was a little heavy-handed, organising that without checking with you first. She just thought it would be a good fit.'

'How, Dad? I've said I don't want to do business and accounting – that's why I dropped out of uni.'

'But you don't seem to have decided on anything else to do.'

'I'm refereeing and coaching football.'

'That's not a career.'

'It could be.' I've raised my voice again, but I need him to understand. I stop. I'm saying things I haven't even worked out in my head 'Maybe I'll train to be a sports coach.'

Dad looks surprised.

'I could do sports science. Or teach PE. Or maybe not. I don't know.' I'm a bit bemused by all the ideas that are just now jumping through my mind. This is something *I* want to do, nothing to do with other people's (Mum's) expectations.

Dad says, 'Probably best not to mention it to your mother until you're sure. She does like to get, er, involved in things.'

'I won't say a word,' I say grimly.

'And you will apologise to her, won't you?'

'If she apologises to me.'

'Jamie, this is your mother's house. You're living here at our expense.'

'So what are you going to do, throw me out?'

'Just apologise to your mother, Jamie.' Dad doesn't lay down the law often. Maybe that's why it's so effective when he does. Also, that wasn't a "no" to my question.

He softens at my expression. 'I know your mother can be difficult at times, but in the absence of rent and utilities, is it too much to ask that you deal with it a little better?'

Ouch. When he puts it like that …

Dad nods like we've agreed on something – which I guess we have. He leaves as calmly as he arrived and I exhale loudly. I think I'll focus on the good that came out of that altercation rather than the possibility of being thrown out on my ass (I'm pretty sure they wouldn't really do that).

I message Gemma.

Jamie: Thanks for your help today.

Gemma: No problem. Not that I helped much.

Sarah did more than me.

Jamie: You were both great. OK for next Tuesday too?

Gemma: Maybe. I'll mention it to Sarah, at least.

I grin. Gemma: always so predictably cautious.

Jamie: I'm going to walk Lucy up in the woods. Want to join me?

Gemma: I should really catch up on school stuff.

Jamie: Just a short walk. Fresh air is good for you.

Gemma: I've been out on a football pitch for most of the afternoon!

Jamie: Exaggeration. Meet me where the paths join in ten minutes? I've got an idea I want to discuss with you.

There's a pause where I'm glaring at the phone, willing her to say yes.

Gemma: OK then. A short walk.

Yes!

Jamie

The next few weeks are manic. Gemma's studying hard in the run-up to her exams, even though she says she doesn't need the results because she still has no idea what she's going to do next year. I accept every reffing opportunity I'm offered and carry on coaching the kids at the primary school. I even arrange a match for them against Kirkdouglas Primary. We lose but I've got high hopes for them in the summer mini league.

Gemma thought the idea of me doing something sports-related in the future was a good one, so I've been looking into that. I was hoping to see her tonight but it's the day after Michael's final exam. He's coming home and Mum has organised a celebratory dinner. She's just about talking to me again after my unreasonable refusal to go for the accountancy interview, and the reluctant apology that followed. She's happy today, excited about seeing Michael.

She doesn't even doubt he'll have passed his exams. Michael isn't the sort who fails.

Maybe being the favourite has its disadvantages. Mum is hanging on his every word and cross-questioning him about every aspect of his life. On the Saturday morning Michael says to me, 'Isn't there a Colts game on today?'

'Probably.'

'You want to go and watch?'

'Can do.' I'd been hoping for a much-needed band practice, but no one's free, and for once I'm not reffing. 'They're on a good run at the moment. I think Kieran Burns, who was in your year at school, is the captain now.'

'I mind Keiran. Bit mental.'

'What you mean is you *remember* Keiran,' says Mum, listening in as usual. One of her life's missions is that Michael and I shouldn't speak with a local dialect.

'I mind,' says Michael, giving her a grin that is bound to win forgiveness, but sliding out of the door to avoid further discussion.

'It'll be good for you boys to do something together,' says Mum. 'I wonder if your father would like to join you ...'

'He'll be playing golf,' I say firmly, and follow Michael before she can try to organise any more of the outing.

'Mum getting you down much?' says Michael as we get into the car.

'All the time.'

'What did you expect?' He's smiling, checking for traffic as he turns onto the main road. He gets to drive because he's the oldest.

'I didn't expect … Actually, I didn't even think it through. I was so desperate to get away from uni.'

'Never could see why you chose to do that course.'

'Thanks for the heads-up. Didn't you think of mentioning it at the time?'

'We've all got to work things out for ourselves.' Maybe Michael is more like Dad than I've realised.

We join the other twenty or so spectators on the sidelines of the Colt's scruffy pitch. It feels good to be here, especially on a warm and sunny day like this.

We stand near a couple of guys I vaguely know. The one whose name I can't remember says, 'You not reffing today?'

I gesture to my jeans and T-shirt. 'Doesn't look like it.'

'Should be a good game. Next to last one of the season. If we win we go top of the league. Pity there aren't more spectators.'

A couple more cars have arrived but that looks like it's going to be it. The other guy, Martin, sighs and says, 'You don't get much of a crowd at games like this.'

The game starts and we're quiet for a while, watching, waiting to see who's going to get the upper hand. The Colts are playing a team from east of Dumfries. They're good, I've taken a few of their games. But they play dirty. I hope Sandy, today's referee, knows what to look out for.

'Foul!' I shout, as someone takes Karl out off the ball. 'That was a blatant foul.'

'Thought you weren't meant to criticise the ref,' says Michael with a snigger. 'Although he must be blind not to have seen that.'

Karl is back on his feet and racing up the park to catch up with play. As he passes the player who felled him he sticks out a leg. The other guy takes a terrific fall and Karl just carries on.

'And it appears the ref didn't see that, either,' says Michael. 'The standards today ...'

'That's the problem with these smaller games, where you only have one match official. You can't see everything.' It feels odd to be watching from the side, but useful too. It gives you a different perspective. Karl is sensibly keeping well away from the guy he just felled and the game settles down.

It ends in a two-two draw, which isn't great for the Colts but better than a loss.

'It all comes down to the last game, then,' says Martin. 'Apparently that'll be Burnsie's last game for the Colts.'

'Really? Where's he going?' Kieran Burns is definitely one of the better Colts players. I can imagine other teams would like to tempt him away, but I'd assumed he'd be loyal.

'He's transferring his apprenticeship to a place in Perth so he'll be living up there.'

Somehow I never saw Burns as the sort of person to leave Newton St Cuthbert. It seems like everyone is moving on except me.

Michael seems to pick up on my mood. As we head back to the car he says, 'You're not planning to stay in Newton St Cuthbert long-term, are you?'

I shrug.

'Thought you were planning to go over to Europe for the summer?'

'It was just a vague idea.' Which I haven't done anything about. 'Actually I'm thinking of applying to work for the council on their summer sports schemes. It'll mean living at home, but I'll be doing stuff I enjoy.' And I'll be able to see more of Gemma.

'You really like coaching the kids?'

'Aye. Weird, isn't it? Never saw myself as a teacher.'

'Don't tell Mum till you're sure,' says Michael. Yes, he is very like Dad. But at least he hasn't shot my idea down either.

Gemma

After my French exam, I decide I need to see Rosie. She hasn't been for any piano lessons since she ran home from football, and Jamie says she hasn't been to any more of the practices either. I'm not even sure she's going to school. I've been too busy to chase about the lessons, and, if I'm honest, too happy. What free time I have I've been spending with Jamie, and things are good with Lily again. It makes me feel that much guiltier about how things ended with Rosie last time.

I pause on the pavement outside her house. It's silent, no sign of life, but it's often like that. Then I see a movement through the sitting room window. I can't turn back now.

Mrs Thomson opens the door. 'Hello, Gemma.'

'Hello. I just, er, wondered ...' Why didn't I plan what I was going to say? 'Is, er, Rosie okay? I'm sorry she hasn't wanted any more piano lessons.'

She looks at me for a long time, the same tired, almost resigned expression. Then a voice calls from inside the house. 'Mum?' Mrs Thomson presses her lips together and nods once. 'Come in and see for yourself.'

She stands back and I follow her reluctantly. What am I about to see? Is something really wrong with Rosie?

If there is, it's nothing obvious. The girl is sitting on the settee, watching cartoons at such a low volume they're practically inaudible. It's a shame for her to be inside on a day like this. She's dressed but her feet are bare. She's pale. I wonder when she was last outside.

'Hey Rosie,' I say.

She huddles into her seat. 'Hello.' She looks at her mum.

Mrs Thomson says, 'Gemma came to ask how you are.'

'I've missed our lessons,' I say brightly. 'Now my exams are nearly over I wondered if you wanted to start again?' Maybe we can pretend that this little hiatus was because I've been so busy, nothing serious. I don't even know if it is serious.

Rosie turns back to the television and says nothing. Her mum raises her voice slightly and says, 'She has been doing some practising. And even trying to play some things by ear. She's doing well.'

'That's excellent,' I say heartily. 'Well, if you change your mind, Rosie, let me know.'

Rosie's head droops and I wonder if she's disappointed that I haven't pressed harder. Should I have? I don't like it when people press me, but sometimes I know I would never have done anything if they hadn't.

Mrs Thomson follows me to the door.

'Thanks for calling by,' she says.

'You're welcome. And I mean it, about teaching Rosie, if she ever wanted to. You don't have to pay me or anything, I really did have fun teaching her.' I want to ask what has happened since I last saw them. Has there been any attempt to get Rosie to see someone who might be able to help her?

'Thank you,' is all Mrs Thomson says.

'Well, goodbye for now.' My jaw feels sore from the constant smiling.

As I leave, I see movement through the window again and wave just in case it's Rosie. The net curtain stills. I tried. But I haven't helped at all. I wanted to get her to do more. Now she's not even coming to piano lessons.

Jamie

One day in late May I get Gemma to take a break from final revision and walk Lucy up in the hills with me. The weather is lovely, warm and dry. I've been doing a bit of sailing but Gemma still point-blank refuses to try that, so walking it is.

'What are your plans for next year?' she says suddenly.

I nudge her. 'Hey, I thought we weren't allowed to ask that.'

'We're both probably thinking about it so we might as well talk about it.'

'I've got an interview for that summer job with the council's sports and leisure department.'

'Coaching football?'

'And other stuff, I presume. I probably won't get it. But I think I've had all I can take of filing at Dad's surgery. And I'm enjoying coaching the kids at football.'

'You'll be able to help coach sailing for this year's regatta.' She grins. 'I should warn you, Lily's already looking for volunteers.'

'That'll be fine. I've been doing some sessions at the sailing club on Sundays.'

'Good.' She nods. 'That's good. You're doing something you enjoy.'

'But I still don't know if I want to make a career out of it. Or even if I can.'

'Of course you can! You can do anything you want to if you set your mind to it – or so my dad always says.'

'But maybe that's just it. Maybe I don't want anything enough.'

She's quiet for a moment, frowning. 'Maybe that's my problem too. Maybe I don't either.'

I take her hand and swing her around before she can get gloomy. 'What a couple of idiots we are.'

'At least you'll be an idiot with a job over the summer.'

'Maybe. And you'll be the idiot with an A in Advanced Higher Music but no idea what to do with it.'

'Ha!' she barks, but she keeps hold of my hand, swinging it as we walk along. It's good to hold her hand. I wish she wasn't so shy when other people are around.

'I did actually enjoy the piano teaching.'

'That still not happening?'

'No. Rosie doesn't want to learn from me anymore.'

'That's not your fault. She's a funny kid.'

'But I wanted to do something. I wanted to make a difference for someone, for once.'

I pull her closer so I can loop my arm around her shoulders and touch my lips to her hair. 'You make a difference to me.'

'Don't be silly.'

She really doesn't believe me. If it hadn't been for her, life back in Newton St Cuthberts would have been miserable. If it hadn't been for her, maybe I wouldn't have thought so hard about my course, about what I actually want to do with my life. It's hard to put that into words so I just say, 'I mean it. I'm really glad you're here.'

She gives me a puzzled glance and begins to walk on. After a silence she says, 'Why me?'

'Why not?'

'I'm not anyone special.'

I sigh. Why does she always have to put herself down? 'Sometimes, Gemma, you just have to get over yourself.'

'Exactly.'

'No, not exactly. Stop saying you're not special. Stop thinking it.'

'But I'm not!' She turns and glares at me, small and flushed. I nearly say, *You are to me,* but that feels a bit scary. Instead I lean in and kiss her. Maybe I can show her like that.

The moment is ruined when Lucy comes rushing back and bounces into a puddle. 'Jesus, that dog!'

I grimace down at the muddy splashes up my legs. Fortunately she got me more than Gemma. 'I'm going to go home and change. Come with me? We've got band practice later anyway. Michael's home so Mum's bound to have baked something.'

I've tried before to persuade Gemma to meet my parents, but she always looks quite panicked at the idea. They must have seen her coming and going to the music room, but they think she's just one of the band. I want them to know she's more.

'I'm not sure ...' says Gemma.

'Please?' I take her hand again and try to look as pleading as Lucy does when she begs. 'For me?'

Gemma shakes her head firmly. I start to sigh, disappointed, then she squeezes my hand.

'Not for you,' she insists, nervous but smiling. 'For *cake.*'

Gemma

Exams are over. Finished! And if I don't go to university, I won't have to do any ever again. It's hard to grasp that amazing thought.

I sit at the piano and start playing some boogie-woogie because there's nothing else I have to do. I quite like jazz but I haven't been able to get anyone else from the band interested. Despite exams we've been managing to practise once a week, and we've finally agreed on a name, Mismatched. I'm quite proud they chose my suggestion.

Preparations for the band night haven't been too bad. Lily, predictably, hasn't been able to stop herself giving advice. Most of it is helpful and when it's not I tell her so, which makes her smile. More than once Tom has given me the thumbs up. I'm pleased they like me asserting myself, and just to show how good I am at it, I rope Tom into helping with the sound system.

Each band is allowed up to five songs. Nobody in Mismatched agreed with my Beatles suggestions so we've decided to start with a David Bowie song. Next we're playing Hurt's 'Wonderful Life', which is actually beautiful. I shouldn't be so dismissive of indie bands. Then one of Jamie's originals, and finishing with 'Heart Heart' so it ends upbeat. For an encore – you guessed it – we'll do 'Ace Of Spades'. But I doubt we'll be doing an encore.

Jamie messages to say he's been offered the summer job with the council. I'm pleased but not at all surprised. Then he asks how my exam went and wants to know if I'll come over. I smile as I reply.

Gemma: OK.

His parents really aren't that bad, at least in small doses. Jamie and I don't talk much about what's going on between us, but things are good. Great, even. Being with him makes me happy.

I cross my fingers. Even thinking that makes me nervous. For now I'll concentrate on the music, and making Mismatched as good as it can be for the band night on Friday.

We're the third band on. Jamie says that's the spot the lead act should take at something like this. First are one of the younger groups, then Mark's band, complete with Mark on bagpipes, who are the most experienced of the lot. The school hall starts off more than half empty and with no atmosphere at all, but

I'm standing in the wings and I can see that people are drifting in all the time. As Lily said, there isn't a lot for teenagers to do on a Friday evening in Newton St Cuthbert.

By the time it's our turn the place is two-thirds full and I'm starting to panic. I thought it would be okay, being part of a band, standing off to the side, no lights on me ... But I'm playing in public, aren't I? And doing backing vocals. My throat seizes up. Why why why did I agree to this?

I have to make an urgent trip to the loo because I think I might be about to throw up. When I come back I say to the others, 'I don't think you really need me. I'll just watch.'

'No way,' says Nathan.

Erin shakes her head. 'I'm not going to be the only girl on stage. None of the other bands have girls.' I don't know why she's worried. She's rocking the music-chick look with tight black trousers and a bandana round her head. We're all wearing black as agreed, but only her and Jamie look good in it.

'You can't back out now,' says Jamie. 'Why would you?'

He doesn't look the least bit nervous himself. He has no idea.

'I–' I can't get any more words out. Why did I think I could do this?

He pats my shoulder. 'You'll be fine once you're on stage. It'll be great.'

And then Lily, who is compèring, announces it's our turn to go on. I want to make a run for it but Jamie grabs my hand and tows me onto the stage. He deposits me before the keyboard, and even gives me a brief kiss. He gets a wolf whistle.

I feel sick. The touch of his lips doesn't help at all. I shift the keyboard closer to the side of the stage. It's already pretty close but I'm nowhere near invisible enough. Suddenly Nathan is counting us in with his stick. I place my fingers on the wrong keys, and we begin.

It's a disaster. I'm completely out of sync with everyone. Jamie turns to look at me and I concentrate and more or less catch up.

After the first song our sound does start to come together. Jamie is grinning, sweaty and delighted. He waves to the audience and they're so into it they shout and wave back. The next number is the one I'm dreading most. It has quite a long bit where the keyboard is playing and no one else, and if that isn't bad enough I'm doing more of a duet with Jamie than just backing vocals. It was okay in the music room at his house. Fun, even.

Here it's just awful. I start off singing in the wrong key and we're probably on the third chorus before I've got it right. As I play the final chords there's a burst of applause, but the thing I hear loudest is laughter. Jamie is looking at me, like he's annoyed at the mess-up. I put up my hands in apology and knock my mic over. The laughter is even louder.

I have to get away. I take a step backwards, and then another. The problem is I've forgotten the stage layout here, or maybe I hadn't realised quite how close to the side I was. There's a kind of corner cut-out for the stairs down into the hall. I lose my footing and with a shriek I tumble backwards down them.

Pandemonium. Nathan knocks over his cymbal stand trying to reach for me, Erin jumps towards me but forgets her guitar is plugged in and stumbles on the lead. Jamie is the only one who stays calm, unlooping his guitar from around his neck before he rushes over to see if I'm okay. Of course, I don't see all of that at the time, but Lily describes it to me later. She thinks it's hysterical.

I've landed in a heap at the foot of the steps. It feels like all of me hurts, but as I scramble to my feet I work out it's just my head, elbow and hip. Worse than that, everyone is staring. 'You okay?' someone shouts.

And then Jamie is there, hauling me up and holding me in place with a hand on each shoulder. 'Jesus! What happened? It was going so well.'

'Sorry. I–'

'Come on. We're losing the atmosphere. Can you get back on stage?'

'Sorry,' I say again, almost in tears.

He looks at me properly. 'You haven't broken anything, have you?'

I shake my head. I'm in a bit of pain but I don't think I'm badly injured. Which I could have been. Steps are notoriously dangerous. I bite my lip and say, 'I'm okay. I just need ...' I look around in desperation.

Lily comes to my rescue. She says to Jamie, 'I'll look after Gem. Can you finish the rest of your set without her?'

'I suppose so. But ...'

'Get back on stage and carry on. Go!' She doesn't give him a chance to argue, just pushes him towards the steps, then hustles me into a side room where pupils aren't normally allowed. It's mostly a store room, but there are a couple of plastic chairs and she pushes me down into one. The door falls shut behind her and I feel immense relief.

Lily shakes her head. 'That was quite some performance. Are you really okay?'

I test my sore places one at a time. It's easier to do that than think about what a fool I've made of myself. 'I'll live.' I wish I had my handbag, I think there's some arnica in there which is good for bruises. I'm definitely going to have a whole load of bruises. I try not to remember the look of disappointment on Jamie's face.

'What on earth were you doing? You know that stage has the stupid cut-out, you've been at school long enough. I've seen one or two close calls but I didn't think you'd be the one to do such a spectacular fall.'

I rub my face with my hands, mostly so I can cover my eyes. 'I wasn't thinking.'

'Clearly. Ah well, you'll be famous after this.' She

starts brushing me down. That floor must be filthy, there's dust all over my clothes.

'I'm such an idiot.'

'It was going quite well until you tried to do a runner. Jamie's better than I expected.'

'And then I spoilt everything.'

'Well, not spoilt, they're still carrying on, aren't they?' I don't answer. After a few minutes she says, 'Do you want to go out and watch the end of the set?'

'No.'

'Come on Gem, I'm not suggesting you go up and join them.'

'I want to go home.'

'You can't do that. This is your band night, remember. You're in charge.'

I stand up. My legs are only slightly shaky. 'I did the arranging. You're the compère. You don't need me anymore.'

'You can't disappear without talking to Jamie.'

Lily's wrong. I saw his face. He was upset. Which he had every right to be. I've completely messed up his big night. But I told him I couldn't do this. He shouldn't have pushed me.

Before Lily can argue any more, I slide out of the room. I don't even go to look for my bag. I just head for home.

Jamie

Our performance isn't bad. It would have been better if Gemma had played the whole set. And definitely better if she hadn't got all those laughs by falling off the stage backwards. 'Heart Heart' doesn't work so well without her doing the backing, but we still had them all dancing. Epic. As we make way for the next act, I'm buzzing.

'Mostly went down well, yeah?'

'Think they liked your song,' says Nathan, looking happy and sweaty.

'I hope Gemma's okay,' says Erin, which brings me back down to earth a bit.

'I'm sure she is. She was more shocked than hurt.' Which means she could have come back on stage if she'd wanted to, but I manage not to say that. 'Lily was looking after her.'

'Well, she isn't now.' We turn and see Lily jumping onto the stage to announce a break before the next act.

I look around properly, the thrill from performing is beginning to die down. If Gemma isn't with Lily she'll be with Tom and Donny. But she isn't. I try to scan the hall, but it's too full for me to spot a tiny redhead. I ignore the backslaps and the comments of "Not bad, mate" and head for Gemma's friends.

Donny says, 'Hey! You were great. Best yet.'

'Thanks. Have you seen Gemma?'

'I think she went home.'

'Aye, Lily said she left,' says Tom, frowning at me.

Donny grins. 'Quite a performance, that. Didn't know she had it in her.'

'It was an accident,' I say shortly. I'm sure he knows that, he's just being an asshole. I go from being annoyed with Gemma for interrupting the performance to feeling bad for her. Poor Gemma. She would have hated all those people seeing her fall. And now she's gone home, so I can't check how she is. Or apologise. I can't remember exactly what I said at the time. I hope I wasn't too unsympathetic.

I send her a message and then hang around while the other bands play, checking them out. This isn't officially a "battle of the bands" so there won't be a winner, but from what people are saying, we probably would have won if there was.

I want to enjoy it, to feel the euphoria that I had on stage, but it's gone along with Gemma. I really wish she'd stayed.

Gemma

I am such an idiot. It's just like at Lily's party: I make a fool of myself, and then without trying to sort things out, I run for home. Should I have stayed? Faced Jamie?

But I couldn't, I really couldn't.

At least Mum and Dad are out so I don't have to explain anything to them. I head up to my bedroom, and then back down to the kitchen to get a drink. I let Toby out. I turn on the television, and then turn it off again. Toby starts barking so I let him in.

What was I thinking, joining a band? Imagining that I could be in a relationship with Jamie? He's not going to forgive me for this. His hope-you're-okay message is half-hearted at best, and I don't blame him.

I don't reply directly. I bring up the Mismatched message group to contact all of them at once.

Gemma: Sorry about that. Hope the rest of the set went well. Wanted to let you know I'm quitting. Good luck for the future.

I press send and then wish I hadn't. I don't regret quitting, but the way I've worded it – way too dramatic. And it isn't like I'm not going to see them again. But it's done now.

School is finished too, apart from the prom which I'm not even sure I'll go to. Luckily I never plucked up the courage to invite Jamie, although I can't deny that I thought about it.

Time to concentrate on getting on with the rest of my life. Maybe I should teach more piano. Although things haven't exactly turned out well with Rosie.

I go to find some arnica and apply it to my bruises. I wonder if the band stuck to our choice of songs and finished off with 'Heart Heart'. They probably did. I hum it to myself. If I say "nothing can bring me down" often enough, maybe I'll believe it.

Jamie

The final band has finished and people are starting to drift away when my phone pings. Gemma answering at last? Except it's a group message and ... *What?*

Nathan and Erin come over. They've read the message too. 'She cannae just leave,' says Nathan.

'We need her,' says Erin. 'She's the really musical one. No offence, Jamie, you're a good performer, but Gemma really knows how to arrange things.'

I don't disagree. 'I'll talk to her. I'll persuade her.'

Unfortunately, Lily's been listening in. 'I think you should give her a break. Perhaps being in your band isn't right for Gem. You must know performing really isn't her thing. If she wants out, then let her make her own decision.'

'But–'

'She felt really bad after that fall.'

'She said she wasn't hurt.'

'Not physically. But she was so embarrassed, Jamie.'

I want to say this has nothing to do with Lily. But what if she's right and persuading Gemma to join the band was the wrong thing to do?

'But she really seemed to enjoy herself at the practices ...'

'Aye, well that's a bit different, isn't it?'

I remember Gemma's reluctance to go on stage, her face, even before the fall, pale and rigid. Did I even tell her how great she sounded?

'Will you talk to Gemma?' Erin asks me.

I'd been planning to head over to Gemma's house right now, but suddenly I'm not so sure. Lily was always the one who encouraged Gemma to do things. If even she thinks I've pushed her too far, maybe I should wait a while?

Gemma

Lily messages to say the band night raised a few hundred pounds. People are already talking about doing it again. I reply:

Gemma: So long as I don't have to be involved.

Between that and Nathan and Erin messaging me not to quit, insisting that my fall really wasn't a big deal, my phone buzzes fairly constantly for an hour before I go to bed. I haven't replied to Jamie and he hasn't messaged again. I feel the first, tiniest little bit of anger. I might have embarrassed him a bit, but I embarrassed myself way more.

I turn my phone off.

I wake up late on Saturday morning, bruised and aching mentally as well as physically. When I finally manage to get dressed, I decide to take Toby for a walk. He hasn't had much exercise recently, and I need to get out of the house. His mournful expression and slow pace are perfect for me.

We inch our way towards the woods. I'm not sure how many more times Toby is going to manage this, but today is bright and sunny and I want him to have a few last happy walks. It's not like I'm in a hurry. I've got the rest of my life to do absolutely nothing.

I brush away my stupid tears and encourage Toby onwards. He sniffs around the trees and trips over roots, but eventually we make it to the pond where Lucy loves to dive for stones. *Don't think about Lucy*, I tell myself.

Toby looks at me hopefully, like he remembers a time when he chased things too. I smile and rub his head.

'You want a stick?' I find a twig and show it to him and then toss it a foot into the shallows. At least, I mean to throw it a foot, but it actually goes much farther.

Toby makes a run forwards, taking us both by surprise. He's immediately up to his stomach in water, and floundering. There's been heavy rain recently and the pond is deeper than I remember. Toby looks back at me in alarm, the stick forgotten.

I step cautiously towards him, my feet sinking in the pond's muddy edge. 'Tobes, this wasn't a good idea. Come on old boy.'

I hesitate.

Even though this water is still, not rushing madly by, not going to pull me in and under, I'm not sure I can take the next steps needed to reach him.

I stretch out my hand and then Toby gives a strange little yelp, and he keels over right before my eyes.

'Toby! Toby! Don't be silly. Don't ...'

I have to get to him. I need to keep his head above water. Yet I'm stuck there in terror, feeling my feet slide deeper. I look at the firm, dry land behind me, then at the spot where he's almost submerged. It isn't far out at all. I can do this. I clamp my teeth together and take a small step, and then another, and reach down into the water.

He's a dead weight of fur and water. I can hardly move him, never mind lift him. I end up on my knees in the muddy shallows, dragging him slowly towards me, ignoring all the expanse of dark water beyond him.

And Toby still isn't moving.

'Toby!' I'm crying now, tears streaming down my face which I try to wipe away with a wet hand. 'Toby.' He just lies there, half across my knees. His eyes are closed and he's completely still. I try to feel his chest. He has to be breathing. He has to be.

Jamie

Gemma isn't answering messages this morning, which doesn't surprise me. I decide to go to her house, something I'd never done before. I really need to talk to her – about the band, about me. Even if she hasn't said she's ending things with me, I know that's what she's thinking.

I take Lucy because it gives me an excuse. When Mrs Anderson opens the door I say, 'Is Gemma in? I wondered if she wanted to, er, walk the dog with me.'

Her mum only takes a second to recognise me. 'Jamie? Nice of you to call by. Gemma's already out, walking Toby. She won't have gone far.'

With that dog, she really won't have. I head back to the woods. It's not long before Lucy's ears prick and she dashes ahead. A little farther and I think I hear the same thing she did. It's not loud but it sounds like crying. I pick up the pace, running into the clearing with the pond and skidding to a stop.

Gemma is on her knees in the water, her face mud-streaked and the dog lying lifeless in her arms.

'I think I've killed Toby,' she sobs as soon as she sees me.

Lucy is already there, sniffing Toby, licking Gemma's face. I take the final steps forwards. 'What happened?'

'Toby just – just collapsed.'

The dog is a ton weight, but I manage to lift him from her arms and lay him down on the undergrowth. He's definitely not moving which makes me feel ill. I turn to Gemma and pull her to her feet. 'Are you okay? You're soaking.' I put my arms around her and pull her close because it's the only thing I can think of to do. She's wailing and shaking and we've got a dead dog lying at our feet. She barely lets me hold her before she steps back. 'We need to get him to a vet.'

'Gem, I don't think a vet …'

'You don't know!' She drops down on her knees and lays her head against Toby's matted side. I'm absolutely sure she'll find no breathing or heartbeat.

'Give me your phone and I'll call your mum.'

'Yes. Yes, good idea.' She fumbles the phone into my hands and leaves me to find her mum in her contacts. I don't think Gemma can face speaking herself.

'Mrs Anderson? No, it's not Gemma, it's Jamie. No, Gemma's fine. It's just, well, Toby …'

I'm so glad when Mrs Anderson takes control. Gemma's dad and brother are home and within five minutes all three have joined us.

'We should call the vet,' Gemma is still saying. She has the dog on her lap again. She's shivering from the wet and cold but doesn't seem to notice.

'I don't think ...' I say for the umpteenth time.

'Here, lass, let me have a look.' Her dad crouches beside her, one hand on her shoulder. Mrs Anderson and her brother hang back.

Her father says, 'It's too late for the vet, Gem. We knew Toby was getting old. Nothing we can do now.'

'He had a good life,' says Mrs Anderson in a broken voice.

Her brother takes off his jacket. 'Wrap him in this and I'll carry him back.'

'It'll make a mess of your jacket ...' says his mum.

'I want to wrap him up. Come on.'

A few minutes later we're all walking back towards the housing estate, Toby wrapped up like a baby who needs keeping warm. Lucy is capering around us, wondering what has happened to her walk. The rest of us are silent except the occasional sniffs from Gemma and her mum.

When we get to the place where our routes part I say, 'I'd probably better, er ...'

Mrs Anderson puts a hand on my arm. 'Thanks for your help.'

'I didn't do anything.'

'I'm glad you were there.'

Her husband nods and then the four of them set off down the last bit of path. I take the turning that leads to my house, stunned by what has happened.

Gemma

I run up to my bedroom so I can cry in peace. I'm nowhere near done when Lily comes over. Messaging her has been the only thing I've managed so far. She plonks herself down on the end of my bed and begins passing me tissues.

'Poor Tobes. I'll miss him too. He was the best dog.'

'He was.' I make myself sit up. 'We're going to do a funeral for him tomorrow. You can come if you want.'

'Thanks, I'll do that. Then afterwards we should go out, do something. We can't have you moping.'

'Maybe.'

She stays for a while and makes me a hot chocolate. It's the only thing she can think of to do. Eventually she hugs me and leaves.

My thoughts go round and round. Dad has phoned the vet to discuss what happened. She says Toby probably died of a heart attack. Dad says there was nothing anyone could have done. I don't believe him though.

Jamie's sent a couple of sympathetic messages, but hasn't suggested he comes round. He's probably had enough of me and all my problems. And I don't even care. I only care that I let Toby down. Why did I throw that stick when I knew he couldn't fetch it? Why am I so scared of water I couldn't even save my dog from a pond?

My phone rings and it's Jamie. I answer it reluctantly.

He says, 'Hi. I was just wondering how you are. I'm really sorry about Toby.'

'Nothing for you to feel sorry about.' It's not his fault, it's mine. And I don't want to talk about it. I don't want to talk to him.

'If there's anything I can do. Maybe if you wanted to get out of the house …'

'No.' I just want to be left alone.

'Maybe we could have a band practice in a couple of days, that would distract you.'

'I've left the band!' I shout. Is that all he can ever think about? 'Why can't you let me be?'

There's a stunned silence on the other end of the phone. I hang up and try to drown my sobs in the pillow.

Gemma

We hold the funeral for Toby in our back garden. It's just as awful as I expected. Lily comes round, and Tom and Sarah too. They've known Toby almost as long as I have. We bury him under the cherry tree, next to the grave of our old cat. As we lay him down in the hole, wrapped in his favourite blanket, it looks like he's asleep. Then Dad lifts the flap over his head and I'll never see Toby again.

Lily tries to jolly us up afterwards, saying we should all go and watch a movie at her place, but I can't face it. I thank them for coming and then say I need to lie down. It doesn't feel like I've been there long, mentally composing a requiem for Toby, when Mum brings someone upstairs. I want to shout *Why can't everyone leave me alone?* when I realise it's Rosie. I can't shout at her.

'Gemma! Is it true about Toby? Oh, Gemma.'

She sits on the on the end of my bed and bursts into tears, so that I have to comfort *her*. That's different enough to rouse me a bit. And I'm worried she's walked here on her own. 'Does your mum know where you are?'

'Yeah. She wanted to come with me but I told her I can go places on my own.'

I suppose that's good news. One bright point in a world of misery. I get Rosie to dry her eyes and take her down to the kitchen for some orange squash.

'I loved Toby,' she says.

'We all did. He was the best dog ever.'

We go through to the music room where I play a few sad bars on the piano one handed. It makes me feel better and Rosie listens quietly.

Then she says, 'I spoke to a woman like you and mum wanted me to.'

I stare at her, confused. It seems like another life when I spoke to Mrs Thomson about Rosie seeing a doctor. Maybe something has come of it. 'That's good.'

'It won't help. She just makes me look at pictures of things and say what I think. That's not going to make me normal, is it?'

'You are normal, Rosie. We're just all normal in different ways.'

Rosie looks doubtful. Not surprising. I'm not sure myself if I've said something insightful or stupid.

'She gave me things to try. Like going out on my own, so I came here.'

'She did that after one meeting?'

'No. I've seen her a few times.' She puts down her

glass. 'I think I'll go home now. I just wanted to tell you I was sorry about Toby.'

'Thanks for coming, I really appreciate it. Shall I walk with you?'

'No. I've got to do things on my own.'

'Okay. But ...' I can see she looks nervous, biting her lip. I want to make everything right for her. Then I think about how I've wanted people to let me make my own decisions; how support is okay but pushing too far isn't. I say, 'If you're happy to walk on your own that's fine, but if you want me to go, I don't know, half way with you, that's okay. Or whatever you want.'

She actually smiles then, that quiet inward smile. It's good to see it after so long. 'Thanks.'

I offer the one thing I can definitely do for her. 'Do you want to start piano lessons again? Maybe tomorrow, or later in the week?'

'Thanks. I – I think I'd like that. I'll have to ask Mum, though.'

I go with her to the door and watch her walk down the street. She's walking quickly, her head down so she doesn't have to make eye contact with the people she might meet walking from our street to hers. At least Rosie's done *something*. I want to follow her example and try and be positive too. But right now I just can't. The loss of Toby is too raw.

Jamie

I've messed up. Gemma was really upset after the band night, but I think maybe I could have talked to her, made things right between us. But then Toby died and I was the first person there and I couldn't do anything to help. I know pets die all the time, but this really got to me. I liked Toby, stupid old dog that he was. And Gemma loved him. I should have left it longer before I phoned, before I pushed to see her. I definitely shouldn't have mentioned the band.

She shouted at me. Gemma *never* shouts. She really doesn't want to see me. And since I can't make things better for her, I should at least do what she wants and leave her alone. I just wish she didn't leave such a huge hole in my life.

Spending time with Mum definitely doesn't make my life any better. Her dissatisfaction only exacerbates mine. Maybe it's taken coming back to live at home, being not exactly happy myself, to make me realise that she isn't that happy either. She keeps busy organising everyone else's lives because I think she's bored sick of her own.

She's going on at me about tidying my room when I say, 'Seriously, Mum, have you ever thought of going back to nursing?'

That certainly stops her in her stride. 'Me? Oh, Jamie, I'm far too old for that.'

'Not necessarily. There's a woman at Dad's practice who's in her fifties and just returned to nursing. She says there's a real shortage of nurses.'

For a moment I think Mum might be interested, but then she shakes her head and asks if I'll be in for dinner, because if so it's her book group night so it'll be early. She says this like the book group is something she's really looking forward to, but somehow I suspect that it's not.

I'm still feeling at a loose end later when she's gone out and Dad is catching up on dictation in his study. I decide to phone Karl. We've had drinks together a couple of times now but that's not what I'm after. 'Have you got Jock Skinner's phone number?' I ask.

'Aye, of course. Why? You wanting to try out for the team?'

'No way. I'm nowhere near good enough. It's just I've heard about this scheme in England where refs go to talk to football teams about the rules. You know, how the game looks from a ref's point of view. D'you think Jock might be interested in me doing that for the Colts?'

'I don't know,' he says. And then, 'Wouldn't harm some of the boys to know what the bloody rules are. It's the end of the season now, though ...'

'I know. But if I planted the idea now, maybe we could start in the autumn.' I don't want to give up. This is my idea, not Mum's, and it fits so well with the football coaching.

'You could give it a go. You want me to sound Jock out?'

'That'd be great. If it worked out with the Colts, I could offer it to other teams. Of course it might turn out to be a crap idea.'

'Won't know until you try it. I'll ask him.'

My spirits lift. It's nothing big, but it's a step in the direction I want to go.

We discuss football some more and agree to meet up for a drink later. The whole crowd are celebrating Burnsie finally quitting his job. Sounds like an okay way to spend the evening to me.

And if I can take the initiative here, I can take the initiative elsewhere too. Tomorrow I'm going to try and get the band back together – what's left of the band. We can't just let it go after one performance.

Gemma

Lily, Tom and Sarah must have decided between them that I've been allowed to mope for long enough. Sarah was here yesterday and Lily's off watching a dancing competition with her mum, so today Tom comes over.

'Final assembly tomorrow,' he announces, like I didn't know and hadn't already decided to give it a miss. We don't have to go and people are probably still sniggering about the band night fiasco. And if anyone even mentions Toby to me ...

Tom continues. 'Lessons are over, exams are finished – we've got the whole summer ahead.'

I gaze out into this unknown future. Even without the loss of Toby, I'd be feeling fragile. The end of whatever it was Jamie and I had between us. The end of school. That's huge. Even for people who've decided what to do next year. Which I haven't.

If Tom's come round to cheer me up, he's doing an extremely bad job of it.

That evening it's Lily's turn. 'Hey, did you see the clips Rory put up of the band night?'

'No,' I say firmly. *Hell no*, is what I mean.

She starts flicking through her phone until she finds what she wants. 'Mismatched were definitely the best. Come on, watch.'

She sticks the screen in my face – Lily's phone is practically a tablet – and I can't avoid watching unless I close my eyes. The video is of our third song, the one I really messed up. Except, as I watch, it doesn't seem that bad.

I do go a bit wrong on the first section, but nobody would know that except Jamie and me. Jamie's voice is good, and I'm coming in with my lines just like we'd practised. We sound fine together. Things only start to go noticeably wrong when I knock over the mic. After that I do close my eyes until Lily takes the phone away.

Lily says, 'Pretty cool, hey? I wish I could sing like that.'

I shake my head, feeling confused. Was the disaster all in my imagination? I'd been sure I was rubbish for my Conservatoire audition too, but that turned out okay.

I don't say anything to Lily. I'll watch the clip again when I'm on my own.

Lily's already moved on to the next thing. 'Come on, let's make the most of the evening sunshine and sit on your swing seat. I'll tell you the latest about the prom.'

I'd completely forgotten about the Sixth Form prom, but Lily hasn't. Possibly because she is the driving force on the organising committee.

'Only nine days to go,' she says in the garden, pushing off with her foot so the rickety seat starts to swing. It makes me feel a bit sick.

I stop it. 'Probably best not to do that, the whole thing might collapse.'

'Shame. I always wanted one of these.' She tries to give it another push, which starts a very disconcerting wobble. 'Uh-oh, maybe you're right. Anyway, you have bought a prom ticket, haven't you?'

'You didn't give me much choice. But I'm not sure I feel like going.'

'It'll be good for you,' she says firmly. 'So now you just need to decide whether you'll bring a date or not.'

I glare. I have no intention of taking a date. 'No date,' I say. 'It's completely archaic thinking that people have to go to these things in pairs. Being on your own is perfectly okay.'

'Of course it is.'

We chat some more, about the decor, which Lily is determined will trounce her efforts from last year, and plans for stopping people being too drunk before they even arrive. We talk about maybe a group of us getting tickets to a local music festival later in the summer. It's good to be with Lily. It's hard to feel like you don't have a future when she sweeps you along on her tide.

Jamie

Karl speaks to Jock Skinner about my ref-talk idea and Jock's all for it. He invites me over for a chat.

'Bloody great idea. We need more kids around like you. Ones who don't bugger off to the big city as soon as the chance arises.'

'Er–'

'I suppose now you're going to tell me you're going off to uni in September?'

'Not this September.' I don't tell him that I don't know what else I might be doing then. The summer coaching job is just that – a summer job. And I'm really not sure I can stand living at home with Mum after that.

'I hear you're helping out with the kids at the primary school.'

'Aye.'

'If you want to improve your coaching skills, you could mebbe do a course at the college in Dumfries.

And they do some great health and fitness courses, too. Got a few of my lads onto them.'

'Do they?' When I'd been at school, I'd been so fixated on getting away from home, I'd never considered studying in Dumfries. I remember Gemma saying you can do primary teaching there. Not that I want to be a primary school teacher. But I could do something that would help me get into sports science, or PE teaching, like I'd mentioned to Dad … 'Sports courses?'

'Aye, they do all sorts these days.'

I'm definitely too late to get on a uni course this year. But if I could do one of these college courses in the meantime, see if I really am interested …

And then Lily of all people comes up with a suggestion that feels as though it's meant to be. We're both down at the sailing club, sorting out the coaching in the run up to the regatta – Gemma was right, she did come after me to volunteer.

'Hey,' she says, marching over once the coaching dates have been agreed. 'Don't you think it'd be good if the gala week included a football competition for the local kids?'

'Doesn't it already?' I'm sure I've reffed at it in previous years.

'It did, but the person organising it has moved away so it's stopped. You know what it's like here, it's always the same people who do everything and without them it all comes crashing down.'

'Surely the Gala Committee can find someone?'

'That's what we're trying to do.'

'I thought you got thrown off the committee?'

'That was last year. We're all great buddies now because basically I'm willing to take on whatever they want. Plus I have these really great ideas.' She grins, so I hope she's being ironic.

'Good for you.' I start to move away. She just moves with me.

'So, I've got Donny's brother Karl to organise the kids' football, him playing for the Colts and everything. And he's agreed to do it, but only if someone else will front it up, do the talking. And who better than you?' She throws her hands wide like she's just performed a magic trick.

'What? I'm already helping with the sailing, and I'm working full-time on the council summer scheme.'

'Which will be during the day, so organising the kids' teams and giving them some coaching can be early evening. Sarah told me you're helping out with the primary school football. You're obviously the perfect person.'

God, I'd forgotten how infuriating Lily could be. And how amazing at getting things done. She smiles happily, ploughing ahead. 'I'll get Karl to give you a phone, okay? And maybe we could rope Jock Skinner in somehow, he could award the trophies at the end. You'll need to decide on age groups and–'

'Lily?'

'Yes?'

'If you want Karl and me to organise this, leave it to us.'

She tosses her head, like she wants to argue. 'Fine. But you'll need to let me know how many trophies you'll want. I'm in charge of ordering those. I think they do quite a good one of a boy balancing a ball on his knee, and–'

'I'll let you know. But it won't be just boys. We'll have girls playing too. Bear that in mind when you order the trophies.'

I leave feeling unreasonably pleased with myself for getting the last word – and bringing in the idea of girls' football. When I get home, Mum is sitting in the kitchen reading a magazine. It's like she's been on pause until I got back.

'How's your day been?' she pounces, which is code for what have I been doing and who was I with?

My mood immediately dips, but I make myself reply. 'I saw Lily down at the sailing club. I'm going to help out with the summer football tournament, as well as with the regatta.'

'You're spending an awful lot of time doing football things.'

'Yes, I am.' Okay, this is it. Here's my chance. I sit down. Clear my throat. 'Actually I'm really enjoying the coaching. I'm thinking of a career in that direction.'

'Football coaching? That's not a career.'

'Sports coaching, sports science – maybe even teaching. It's something I'm thinking about. I can't get into uni for the coming year, so I'm thinking about doing some courses at college, see if I really am interested.'

'The college in Dumfries?'

'Yes.' I sit forwards. Since that chat with Jock I've checked out exactly what courses are on offer. And I've been thinking about Mum, too. I've had an idea about something she might like to do. 'Did you know they also do nursing courses there? They offer refreshers for people who've been out of the profession for a while. People like you.'

She looks bemused by the subject shift, but this time she doesn't dismiss the nursing idea outright. 'Do they really? So close?'

'Yeah. It'd be handy for you, wouldn't it?'

'I don't know. I'd have to discuss it with your father ...'

'Oh he wouldn't mind.' I bet Michael wouldn't either. It would definitely get her off our backs. Although that's not the only reason I'm suggesting it. Mostly I just what her to be happy.

'You should think about it, Mum,' I say. 'I'll send you the link to their website and you can have a look.'

I'm guessing from the thoughtful expression on her face that she might be taking this seriously. Which has the added benefit that she doesn't ask more about my college plans. She sits there, nodding and then shaking her head to herself. I leave her with whatever dreams she's having of her own future, and go off to get on with mine – hopefully with a little less interference.

Gemma

Mum says, 'Do you want to go shopping for a prom dress?'

I've left it really late. The dance is this Friday and I still can't decide whether to go or not, but Mum hasn't given up.

She says, 'I mentioned to Lesley that we might go into Dumfries and Sarah asked if she could come along to get some new jeans. I think she'd just appreciate the trip.'

I can see she's not going to let me wriggle my way out of this. 'Okay.'

As we near Dumfries the road crosses the River Nith more than once, and the waters look high and dangerous. 'I wonder if the Whitesands will be flooded,' says Mum, sounding more curious than concerned. It isn't flooded so we park in the car park close to the river and Sarah goes to peer over the railings. The water rushes by in swirls of brown.

'Kind of mesmerising,' she says.

I've kept a step back, but now I make myself stand beside her. I need to get over my stupid fear, even if it's too late for Toby. I place my hands on the metal railings and lean right over.

'Watch out!' says Sarah, grabbing my arm. 'I know it kind of draws you in, but I don't think you really want to go there.'

'I'm trying not to be so scared.'

'Well, maybe try some time when there hasn't been so much rain? Come on, your Mum's waiting for us.'

Shopping is not one of my strengths. We finally manage to get some jeans that fit Sarah. She's delighted to find she's put on weight and has gone up a size. Not many people would be cheering about that. Then I see a charity shop with two ballgowns in the window.

'Let's have a look in here.'

'You never get anything to fit you in these places,' says Sarah.

'We won't know until we try,' says Mum. I think she's just grateful I'm showing the slightest bit of interest.

And the silky jade dress has caught my fancy. It's got an off-the-shoulder neck with tiny spaghetti straps to make sure it doesn't fall down. The material catches the light in a really pretty way.

'We've had lots of people interested in that,' says the shop assistant, taking it out of the window. 'Such a shame it's a petite six so it hardly fits anyone.'

'But it might be just perfect for Gemma,' says

Mum, taking the dress and hurrying me towards the changing room at the back of the shop before I can change my mind.

I really hate trying stuff on, especially second-hand things, but I hear the lady telling Mum the previous owner had the dress dry-cleaned and how it's quite a well-known brand but they've had to reduce the price because of the size.

I stop listening as I pull the fabric over my head and let it settle over what curves I have. A girl stares out at me from the mirror with startled eyes. This dress is stunning. Maybe a tiny bit loose, but Mum's good at minor alterations. I turn all the way round, watching the bodice sparkle under the shop's fluorescent lights, the skirt swirling out.

'Well?' says Sarah outside the curtain.

'Can I come in?' says Mum.

I step out. 'I think this one might do.'

'Oh wow,' says Sarah softly.

'Perfect,' says Mum with the broadest of smiles. 'I knew we'd find something eventually. You look beautiful.'

'It might need a bit of altering,' I say. I'm not used to praise for my appearance. I have no idea how to react to it, even if I'm pleased.

It's only as we're driving back to Newton St Cuthbert that I remember I hadn't actually decided whether I was going to the prom or not. Now that I have the perfect dress, it looks like I am.

Jamie

I've got into the swing of doing the kids' football at the primary school. There aren't as many attendees as on the first couple of weeks, but there are enough to make it worthwhile. I'm glad that four or five girls have kept on coming, and Sarah sometimes comes along to help out. I think it depends on how well she's feeling, but as summer approaches and the weather warms up, she's there more often than not.

No sign of Gemma, of course. I know she isn't really into football. Or me, anymore. Or the band, even. But it's like she's disappeared off the face of the planet. The sixth years have finished school so maybe she's gone away like Erin has, which means we can't have a band practice even if Gemma had been willing. I know it's the prom this Friday, though, and surely she'll be around for that?

I haven't chased her to spend time with me. I got the message. I'd just like to know she's okay. I think about mentioning her to Sarah, who's helping with the football today, but that seems a bit needy. And then someone else catches my attention.

'Rosie?' I stroll over and nod to her. 'Good to see you back. Let's check your footwear. Yeah, that seems fine. Join in with these three here and start the passing, okay?'

She goes to join in. The other kids know the drill now and start the practice routines without being told. After they've had a bit of fun improving their ball skills, I set them to running around the field a couple of times. Surprisingly, Rosie is at the front this time.

'She's a good runner,' I say to Sarah who is watching them with me.

'Who, Rosie?' We both watch as she covers the ground with a long, loping stride. 'I suppose she's got the build for it, tall and skinny. Although I never really thought of her as sporty.'

'I didn't think she'd come back here again after running off that time.'

'I suggested it to her when I saw her at Gemma's.'

My heart gives a stupid little kick at the mention of Gemma's name. 'Rosie's gone back to doing piano?'

'Apparently.'

'Gemma will be pleased.' This is as near as I can get to a question about Gemma.

'Very.'

The youngsters come trailing in after their second circuit and I have to get back to them. At the end Rosie hangs around, waiting for Sarah. Sarah asks her to help collect the bibs and pile up the cones, which she does without saying a word.

I see Mrs McQuarrie, the head teacher, heading over to talk to us and my heart sinks. She normally just lets us get on, which is the way I prefer it. People only come and talk to you when they want something.

'Thanks for doing this Jamie, we really appreciate your help,' she says.

'No problem. I'm enjoying it. And Sarah helps, too.'

'That's kind of you, Sarah.' She gives Sarah that extra-warm smile that people often give someone they think isn't quite up to strength. I bet that's really annoying.

'I was wondering,' says Mrs McQuarrie. Ah ha, here it comes … 'We're having our sports day in a couple of weeks, and I was wondering if you might help out? It'll be more fun for the children if we have someone different doing the starting, awarding the medals, things like that.'

'I'll help out if I can.' There's really no easy way of getting out of it. And it might be good experience.

One of the girls comes up and tugs on Mrs McQuarrie's arm. 'Mum, Mum, are we doing sports day in houses? Rosie's in my house, isn't she? She's really good at running. Can we do the competitions in houses?'

'I don't see why not.' Mrs McQuarrie looks at Rosie who's folding away bibs, and then at me, her eyebrows raised. 'A runner?'

I nod. 'I think she could be a good one, with a bit of encouragement.'

'I'll add her to my list.' Mrs McQuarrie beams and goes over to speak to the silent girl, who looks up and nods before returning her gaze to the bibs.

'I used to be good at running,' says Sarah.

'Maybe it's time you took it up again,' I say. I'm not going to be the one to pussyfoot around her. 'Why not? You and Rosie could train together, be good for both of you.'

'I don't think ...' Then she pauses, pushing her glasses further up her nose. 'Well, who knows? Maybe I can. I'll talk to Gemma. We can work on Rosie together.'

'That's a good idea.' I wonder if I can make this a reason for going to see Gemma myself, but I can't quite work out how.

Gemma

I thought I was doing well, getting over losing Toby.
Then, the day after we buy the dress, Mum says how
great it is that I'm going to the prom and maybe it
will help me forget, which makes me cry so hard I can
hardly see. How can she think I'd want to forget?

'I want him to still be here,' I say, probably
incoherently. She hugs me and sighs.

The next evening after dinner Dad joins me in the
kitchen where I'm washing up.

'I'll dry,' he says, which is how I know he's come in
to speak to me. Offering to help with household chores
is not Dad's style. He picks up the tea towel and for a
minute or two we process the dishes in silence.

He says eventually, 'What are you planning to do
with all the free time you have now?'

I sigh. The real answer is nothing. 'I haven't decided
yet. Lily's got some ideas.'

'Be good for you to get out a bit more, do things.'

I stare at him. Dad doesn't normally push me to "do things". He understands that I'm not outgoing. 'I'm serious, Gemma,' he says now. 'You need to stop obsessing over Toby and using it as an excuse to hide away.'

I take my hands out of the water so I can turn and glare. 'I'm not obsessing over Toby!'

'I think you're still blaming yourself. Toby was old, Gemma. He had to die at some point. We were lucky to have had him so long, we need to remember the good times. I'm sorry you were on your own when he died, but it wasn't your fault.'

'I know that.'

'Do you really?'

'Yes,' I say. 'Really.' It took me a while to see that what everyone said was true, but I accept it now. Even if a little part of me still feels guilty.

'Good then. Time to move forwards, yes? And you don't need to wait on Lily for ideas, I'm sure you'll come up with some of your own.'

He gives me a hug, and then leaves me to finish the pans on my own. His words have made me feel better. Tearful and a little nervous, but better. Dad only says what he actually believes, and he only makes an effort to speak if it's important.

Dad's words stick with me all evening. The more I think about it, the more I realise he's right; it really is time for me to move forward.

I suspect that means making some decisions.

I've got to stop avoiding everything. It's like I look for excuses not to do things. Leaving the band because I fell off the stage. Ignoring Jamie because I was upset about Toby.

I'm going to make a list.

Things I've Been Avoiding, Number One: What am I going to do next year? I think about all the courses I applied to and one thing becomes very clear: I don't want to do any of them. I don't want to go away. I don't want to study music further. And I don't know what I *do* want to do, so I'm going to make a positive decision to give myself more time. I go online and decline them all.

Doing that down gives me a huge sense of relief. I don't have to decide on the rest of my life right now. How amazing is that?

Things I've Been Avoiding, Number Two: I still need a plan for the summer. I can help Lily with gala stuff again, but I really need to think about earning some money. I haven't applied for any jobs, but maybe I don't need to. Why don't I give more piano lessons? I've no excuse about being too busy now. And I have come to enjoy them. I send off a message to Mrs Marshall.

I'm feeling a bit shaky now, with all these decisions. But shaky in a good way. Excited shaky. So, Number Three: The water. I told Lily that my fear wasn't holding me back, but I don't believe that anymore. Maybe it wouldn't have saved Toby, but what if something like this happens again? I should be able to get wet without freaking out. I take a deep breath and message Lily to say I'm up for another visit to the spa some time very soon.

There's one last thing, but it doesn't depend entirely on me.

The prom.

I have the dress. I have the shoes – impractically high and silver. I even have a tiny silver bag. All I'm missing is a partner. I know I don't *need* a partner, but there's one I want.

It's weird to think that Jamie was Lily's boyfriend last year and now he's … well he was sort of *my* boyfriend until I panicked and opted out. Things ending between us wasn't his fault. Well, it wasn't totally his fault. He was impatient with me, but it wasn't his fault I thought I'd done so much worse than I had. And he did apologise. I was being an idiot as usual, refusing to talk things out.

And then poor Toby died and I couldn't think about anything else, or if I did think about Jamie it was of him finding me with Toby in my arms. But Dad's right. I need to concentrate on the good memories. I have lots of those. Of Toby. And of Jamie.

I miss having him in my life. My feelings for Jamie are one of the few things I've always been sure about. Even as I've got to know him better, and found he isn't the confident, successful person I thought he was, my feelings haven't changed. I only really doubted that he could possibly like me back. And yet he did. Sarah said it seemed like he wanted to talk about me at football practice. It's me who's been pushing him away. I even shouted at him on the phone!

Have I pushed him too far? I'm not sure he'll come to the prom even if I invite him. But I won't know unless I ask him, will I?

My hand hovers over the phone. Should I message or call? Or should I go to his house, speak to him in person? Finally I call.

'Gemma?' he answers. 'You okay?'

'Why wouldn't I be?'

'We haven't spoken for … a while.'

'No, I suppose … No ….' Then there's silence while he waits for me to say why I'm calling and I can't find the words.

'Gemma, you still there?'

'Yeah. Er, look.' I take a deep breath. 'I wondered … Are you doing anything on Friday?'

'This Friday?'

'Yes. It's the prom. Which you probably know. And I wondered if you wanted to go. With me. But if you're busy, that's fine.'

This time he's the one who's silent.

'Jamie?' I say, my voice high-pitched.

He says slowly, 'You're asking me to prom?'

'Well, yes. But if you don't want to …'

'Well I'll have to check my calendar, but if I find I'm free …' He trails off, leaving another silence that I can't fill. 'Gemma, of course I'd love to come.'

'Thanks' I say. 'Gosh. Thanks.' *He said yes!*

I tell him what time prom starts and he asks if he should wear a kilt or a suit.

'A kilt,' I say, forgetting my nerves completely. 'You look good in a kilt.'

At that he laughs and I grin sheepishly. Did I really just say that?

He says he'll pick me up at seven o'clock, and we chat a little more before hanging up. I feel light-headed with excitement. I did it. I asked Jamie to prom.

Now I just need to let Lily know I need an extra ticket. Oops – perhaps I should have thought of that before I invited Jamie? I take another deep breath and phone her. 'Hi Lils.'

'Hi you. Decided whether you're going to come and get ready for the prom at my place?'

'No, I don't think so. Er, Lily?'

'Yeah?'

'You know you said there were a couple of tickets left?'

'Aye.'

'So, well, I'm going to need one.'

She's gives a little screech. 'You're going to invite Jamie? Go you!'

I grin. 'I already have, so I'm relieved you actually do have a ticket.'

'I do indeed. And if I didn't, I'd create another one just for you. Well done you. I'm so pleased.'

'Thanks.'

When the conversation ends, I drop the phone onto my bed and fall back against the pillows. That all went pretty well. Maybe making decisions isn't as difficult as I thought it was?

Gemma

I'm so nervous getting ready for prom that I have to ask Sarah to come over and do my make-up. I don't want to arrive looking like a panda, which is what happened both times I tried to apply eyeliner myself.

'I love this dress,' says Sarah approvingly.

'Really? Do you think it's okay?' I frown down at my shoulders. 'I'm so glad it's got the straps to make sure it doesn't fall off. I do not want to be one of those girls whose dress slips lower and lower as the evening goes on.'

'No wardrobe malfunctions for you,' says Sarah.

She faffs around correcting my eyeliner and sweeping on some blusher. Finally we decide that my face looks as good as it's going to. Now for my hair.

'I'm so jealous of your hair, it's such a nice colour,' Sarah says as I try for the fifth time to put it up in a secure but messy bun. 'Looking good,' she says, when I've succeeded, standing back to look me up and down.

'And it's nearly seven o'clock. Better put your shoes on then you're ready to go.'

'Oh god,' I say. 'Why am I doing this?'

'Because it's going to be fun. I hope I get to go to prom one day.'

'I hope so too,' I say, momentarily distracted. 'Here's you pleased to be going back to school next year, and I'm just happy it's finished!'

'It's not definite I'm going back.'

'I think you will.' I hope she will.

Just then we hear the car pulling up outside and Sarah hustles me downstairs to be admired by Mum and Dad, and ready to slip out of the front door as soon as Jamie knocks.

Jamie

Gemma looks stunning. I'm about to say so when I realise she's white beneath the make-up and her hands are shaking as she grips a tiny bag.

So I just smile and say a brief goodbye to her parents before taking one hand. 'Your carriage awaits – aka Dad's Audi.'

If Gemma notices the joke she doesn't let on.

'Oh,' she gasps, the second we pull away from the kerb. 'I've just thought, what if you want to drink? I should have got Dad to take us.'

'I don't think we want your dad along. And if I do have a drink, we can get a taxi back and I'll pick up the car tomorrow. No problem.'

'Okay.' She sits back in her seat, but I can see she's chewing the inside of her lip, looking for the next difficulty. It's like she's regretting this already.

As soon as we get outside the town, I pull the car into a layby. I turn off the engine and take her hand.

I've been missing her for weeks, but if she thinks this is a mistake, I'll just have to respect that. 'Are you okay? You know if you don't want to go to the prom, we don't have to.'

'Lily would never forgive me.'

'Forget Lily. It's your life.'

She watches me silently, her light blue eyes scanning my face, and then down over both our outfits. 'We have to go, we've both made so much effort.'

'But do you want to?'

She nods slowly and then again more firmly. 'Yes. Yes, I do. I'm just nervous. But I'm trying to do things even if they do make me nervous. And you only get one chance to go to your school prom, don't you?'

'Well thanks to you I get two chances.'

'No, you don't. Last year was your prom. This year is mine. And it's going to be fun.'

She looks fierce in her determination and I can't resist. I lean in, placing a soft kiss on her lips. 'Thank you for inviting me.'

'Hey, don't mess up my lipstick!'

She's laughing so I pull her close for a moment, kissing her neck and feeling her slightness and her warmth, smelling the scent of Gemma.

Then I let go. 'Okay, shall we go do this thing?'

'Yep, let's do it.' She's still laughing. I've managed to relax her. It's going to be fine.

It feels kind of weird to be going to a prom again, exactly a year after the one I went to with Lily. Back when I was head boy and still trying to be the son Mum wanted me to be. Now I just need to be Gemma's partner, and that sounds bloody brilliant to me.

Gemma

When we arrive, Molly Douglas is doing a commentary like a red-carpet fashion critic: 'Look at Suzie! Lovely dress, great hair, HORRIBLE fake tan. Should've exfoliated first. And Erin, wow, stunning dress, no effort with hair. Gemma! You're … *here*. Hey, are you two together? I heard about that kiss on stage …' I take Jamie's arm and pull him past her.

'Sorry. Looking for Lily,' I say firmly.

I find her talking to the photographer, but she swings around when she sees us.

'Gemma! You look amazing. Love the dress.' She hugs me and I feel her chin against my shoulder as she nods at Jamie. 'Looking good, dude.'

'Not so bad yourself.' He takes my hand, like he wants everyone to know we're together.

I can feel myself blushing. 'I hope the photos aren't going to take long. I could really do with a drink.'

Lily claps her hands. 'Right, best get them started

then. Everyone, up on the steps please …'

I pull Jamie to the side and back of the crowd, hoping that there'll be very little of me visible on the group photo. I'm doing well. I'm here with Jamie. I'm happy. But I don't have to like having my photo taken too, do I?

The evening is pretty good. Everyone looks lovely, but to me Lily is especially beautiful. She's in a red dress which goes brilliantly with her dark hair.

'You look great,' I say when she eventually comes to sit down.

'You've scrubbed up pretty well yourself. And don't the boys look good?'

We turn to admire them. Tom and Donny and Ricky are all in suits, but Jamie totally overshadows them in his full kilt outfit: green and red tartan, pristine white shirt, black jacket, socks with tartan flashes. It really suits him. Or maybe I'm just biased?

After the food, the lights dim and the music starts.

Jamie takes my hand, 'Come and dance.'

I don't resist. This is our evening. We're here as a couple. We're meant to be dancing together. So what if people stare?

We dance for three or four numbers and are heading back to our seats when the first notes of 'Heart Heart' begin to play. I tug Jamie to a halt. 'Come on, we have to dance this. It's practically our song.'

'Our song?'

'Our band's song.'

'So you're still in the band?' He's grinning.

'Shut up and dance.'

We turn back and are in time for the first mighty chorus. Lily smiles on us like some kind of fond godmother. She and Tom have danced nearly every number so far. Her dancing has definitely improved. Donny can't keep a smile off his face. He sits out some of the dances with Ricky, preferring the slow dances when they do join in. Lily has been on the lookout for anyone making untoward comments about the first same-sex couple to attend our prom. I think she's secretly a bit disappointed that no one is paying any attention at all. To me that's how it should be.

Jamie only has one beer early in the evening so he says he's fine to drive us home. I remember last year Lily said he wanted to stay to the very end, say goodbye to everyone. But he was head boy then and he isn't now. We leave all that stuff to Lily and Rory (who isn't being particularly helpful) and head off just before one. I'm tired, but in that hazy, dreamy kind of way where everything feels only half-real.

'It seems a shame to go straight home,' says Jamie. 'Let's go for a walk. Maybe down by the river?'

My stomach clutches at the thought of the river in near-darkness. I make myself say, 'Okay, why not? As long as I can walk bare foot.' I'd kicked off my shoes as soon as we got into the car. I don't think I could get them back on now if I tried.

'You should be okay walking on the grass.'

Jamie parks on the edge of town and when I start to complain about the gravel I'll need to cross to get to the path he swings me into his arms.

'Careful!'

'Like I'm going to drop you.' He hoists me higher for good measure and pushes his way through the latch gate. Then he puts me down gently on the grass already cold with dew. I can't prevent a shiver. He puts his arm around me. 'Do you want my jacket?'

'No. It's just my feet – and no I do not want your socks!'

He closes his mouth with a grin.

We begin to walk slowly upstream, the light of the full moon reflecting on the water so that it almost doesn't look threatening. I move so that I'm on Jamie's other side, the one nearest the water. I keep hold of his hand.

'I'm going to take up swimming,' I say.

'Really?'

'And maybe sailing. Or rowing. I'm going to do all the stuff I want to do but haven't before because I was scared. I might even book in for my driving test.'

'That sounds good,' he says.

We walk on for a while, the only sounds the rush of the water below us and an occasional bird or small animal rustling through the bushes. When we reach a bench that looks out over a bend in the river, we sit down without even speaking.

I turn to Jamie and he turns at the same moment. We kiss. It's not like the first kiss. We know each other now. I'm not nervous. I lean in, putting my hands up to his gorgeous, wavy hair, wanting more of him, all of him. When we eventually pull apart, I'm feeling dizzy.

I lean my head back against his shoulder, looking up at the starry sky. It's beautiful here. Anything seems possible. 'Did I tell you about Rosie?' I ask.

'Huh?' Clearly this wasn't the direction he thought the conversation would go in.

'She's been seeing a psychologist and she's started coming back for piano lessons. She's probably always going to find life a bit difficult, but she's learning ways to cope.'

'That's good. And I bet part of it is down to you.'

I think about it and nod. I didn't do much for Rosie, but I am doing *something*. 'I'm going to take on some of the other kids Mrs Marshall has been going on at me about. It won't be many but I'll be earning some money and using my music. Mum and Dad are happy for me to live at home and do that until I decide if I want to do something else.' It feels good to be saying my plans out loud. 'And there's a chance I could go to the Musicians' Centre that Mrs Gurthrie has been going on about, to do a course on improving my teaching skills. Just a short course, but it might be good.' Goodness, did I really say that?

'Sounds brilliant. I bet you're a great teacher.' He hugs me closer. 'I've enrolled for a couple of sports courses at the college, so we're both sorted for the next wee while. The rest we can figure out as we go along.'

He opens his mouth to continue but I put a finger to his lips to stop him. I have more to say.

'Jamie, I'd like to go out with you. Properly.' Almost immediately, the uncertainty I was barely tamping down begins to rise. 'Of course, if you don't want …'

'I want,' he says, removing my fingers and kissing them briefly. 'I want to go out with you. *Properly*, as you say.'

'It might not last, who knows … But right now, I *really* want to go out with you.'

'If you're sure,' he says, laughing.

And I laugh back. Who knows what the future holds? Not us. Except that it'll be scary and surprising and, maybe, fun.

'I'm sure.'

ACKNOWLEDGEMENTS

Writing *Gemma's Not Sure* was great fun, but also occasionally difficult because some aspects of the main characters are quite distant from my own experience. I am, to my great disappointment, not at all musical. Enormous thanks are therefore due to Ailish Oldfield, Darcy Howat and Cecilia Bennett for sharing with me their memories of music practices, exams and college applications. Likewise, I have never played football, let alone worked as a football referee (although I love watching the game). I owe a huge debt of gratitude to Robert Peacock for patiently talking me through the intricacies of being a young football referee in Scotland. In all cases, the responsibility for any errors is entirely my own.

Many thanks to my very patient editors, and to everyone at Sweet Cherry Publishing for their input and creativity.

Huge gratitude to my two (two!) agents, Kate and Lina, of Kate Nash Literary Agency, who are always a joy to work with.

Thanks also to my writing buddies for their support and encouragement, and for the fantastic Romantic Novelists' Association for giving me the opportunity to make many of these friends.

Finally, thanks to my family and friends who have put up with my endless complaints about needing to do some writing, but not being able to get round to it. You gave me the space so that I did, eventually, get round to it!